I0457597

ZARA'S ZEPHYR

JANELLE DANIELS

Dream Cache Publishing

Zara Wigg is a dreamer. So, when she's offered the chance to build her own school and become a mail-order bride, she agrees to all conditions—including the one about taking a husband. But when she arrives in Promise Creek and discovers the man she's fallen in love with through letters isn't her intended, those dreams collapse.

Thaddeus Gray has one goal: to strike it rich. His sole focus has been on his gold mine, but after writing letters to someone else's bride, life takes a turn. The woman he wrote to is the only one he's ever seen a future with, but any relationship with her is impossible. When her engagement dissolves and she's left in a precarious position, he steps in to help her, regardless of the personal cost.

As word gets out of her need for a husband in the woman-hungry town, chaos erupts. Thaddeus is thrown into the position of protector and matchmaker, but as her deadline to marry approaches, he must decide which is more important...love or gold

To sign up for Janelle Daniels' readers club and receive notice of new titles as they are available, go to
www.janelledaniels.com

To the other authors of The Alphabet Mail-Order Brides. Thanks for being such great friends!

CHAPTER 1

It wasn't Zara Wigg's fault real life was so boring. At least, it *used* to be. Her body practically vibrated with excited energy as she packed the last of her trunks.

She swiveled around, placed a hand on her hip, and grinned at Yetta, her roommate in the foundling home. "Done! I'm all done!"

Yetta closed the book she was reading and placed it next to her on her bed. Her trunks were already packed and stacked along the wall. "Good. I was starting to worry you wouldn't be ready in time. You're the last one, and we're leaving tomorrow."

Zara swatted away Yetta's concern. "I wasn't worried. There were too many other things to do. Besides, I packed the truly important things early."

"You mean your books on Greek culture and mythology?"

Zara answered in Greek. "Akrivos." *Exactly.*

Yetta chuckled. "Your husband better be a patient man."

"Oh, he is." She thought of the two letters they'd exchanged, tucked safely in one of her trunks. He'd written to her with passion and eloquence. Even his penmanship was impeccable. He craved success and living life to the fullest—two qualities she appreciated in a man.

When she'd spoken of Persephone, his answer about Hades instantly falling in love had thrilled her. "He's perfect," she added.

"Zara..." Yetta trailed off her warning, but Zara knew what she was thinking. Yetta was just as hopeful about becoming a mail-order bride, but she was also reserved. Zara had no desire to temper her excitement with worry though. Becoming a mail-order bride was just like all the romantic adventures she'd read about.

Oh, she knew what everyone at the orphanage thought of her. She had her head in the clouds, preferring dreams over the cold, hard facts of reality. She sometimes neglected her daily chores, but only because she didn't find them important —*not* because she'd forgotten about them.

Who wanted to polish scuffed boots when they could read about heroes, gods, goddesses, and warriors? Why worry over dust bunnies under her bed when she could sit amongst the roses in the foundling home's small garden, imagining the man who would win her heart? Those things were far more fascinating than what real life had to offer.

Each of the older girls taught varying subjects to the younger orphans in the home. They worked, learned, and took care of one another. But all that was about to change. "Are you more excited to meet your husband or start your school?" Zara asked.

A smile spread across Yetta's face. "He seems like a good man, and there's definitely a need for a school where he is, so I'm looking forward to that." Her look turned serious. "I just wish Wiggie were well and we were leaving under different circumstances."

Zara wished the same. When Wiggie had told them she was dying, it had broken her heart. Their guardian had always been a pillar of strength, and it would gut her to lose the only mother she'd ever known.

Yetta would be the perfect teacher, just as Wiggie had been. She was tough when needed but had a huge heart. The children in Colorado were lucky. "You're going to enrich so many lives."

"I hope so." Yetta smiled as if already imagining it.

Zara wanted the same. When Vera Mae, Wendi, Yetta, and herself had approached Wiggie, insisting they be given the same opportunity as the older girls to become mail-order brides and start their own school, Zara hadn't been sure their guardian would allow it. They were the youngest, but there was no doubt in Zara's mind she was ready for this adventure.

Wiggie loved them, and they'd formed their own sort of family, but they'd all had hardships, growing up as orphans. Each of them had overcome challenges and had grown into the people they were meant to become. Plus, with Wiggie's prognosis, she'd agreed it was best to get the girls settled.

Zara ran a hand over her trunk, the few dresses and belongings she owned tucked inside. "It's hard to believe I'll be in Montana so soon. Away from everyone."

Yetta stood from the bed and walked over. "It's not so very far from Colorado. Just a short train ride. Plus, we can write each other. Every day if we want."

"We'll beggar our husbands."

Yetta shrugged. "They'll manage." They both giggled.

Zara was beyond excited, but a hint of nerves was there too. "I promise I'll write as often as I can." Not wanting Yetta to worry, she winked. "That is, if my husband can stand to let me go for more than five minutes."

Yetta rolled her eyes with a snort. "I just hope he's every-thing you dream him to be."

Zara did too. She refused to think otherwise. "He will be. And so will yours. We're the luckiest women in the world."

A knock sounded at the door, and Zara smiled, guessing who it was. "Come in."

Vera Mae and Wendi walked in, their faces serious, as if they'd come to help her pack. But they relaxed once they saw her stacked belongings. "You're done," Vera Mae said, unable to completely mask the surprise in her voice.

Zara smiled ruefully. "You know, I do manage to get things done when I need to. When it's *important*."

The others rolled their eyes and laughed. "Well, we weren't completely confident you'd have it finished," Wendi said. "We were happy to help."

"I appreciate the thought." Zara patted her closed trunk. "But I managed." Seeing them all together, the last group to leave, was bittersweet. "This is it. The last night we'll be together here."

"Don't say that." Yetta groaned. "You're going to make us all cry."

Vera Mae sniffled, and Wendi blinked a few extra times.

"All right." Zara held out her hands, and they took them, standing in a circle. "I won't say it. But I'm thinking it. We're about to set off on an adventure. One that will change our lives forever."

Vera Mae cleared her throat. "That isn't helping."

Zara snorted. "Regardless, it's true. I just know we're going to be so happy. This was the right thing."

They all nodded in agreement. No matter what, no matter how different they were, they all felt the same.

Everything would turn out as Zara hoped. She just knew it.

THADDEUS GRAY WAS HUNGRY. BUT NOT FOR FOOD. HE

was driven, ambitious, and willing to work until his fingers bled if it meant his gold mine paid out.

He was close. So close, he could feel it. It was one of those things the other men in town talked about, the ones who had hit their mother lodes. They could *feel* they were close.

And everything within Thaddeus was tingling.

It was still early, but he'd taken the rest of the day off to regroup, to map out a plan. He didn't dare draw a physical map though. Besides, he didn't need one. Every tunnel, every nook and cranny, was emblazoned in his memory. He knew where he'd searched, where shafts dwindled to nothingness. There were three areas he could search next. One had to hold the main vein.

He blew out a breath and scrubbed his face with his hand before signaling a waiter to his table in the main dining room at the Promise Creek Hotel. The man whisked over to him with a deferential nod. "Your usual, Mr. Gray?"

"Yes. Thank you."

The man nodded again. "It will be out shortly," he said.

The service at the Promise Creek Hotel couldn't be beat. Ever since Winthrop Hotels had taken over the establishment, it was in a class of its own.

Thaddeus' mine produced enough to afford such luxuries, and he didn't bother squirreling his money away for hard times. He knew there was more, *much more*. All he had to do was find it. Until then, he'd enjoy the small luxuries Promise Creek had to offer.

He'd grown up poor, and he didn't take his small amount of wealth for granted. Pretty soon, he'd have the means to buy a place just like this, if he wanted. He could travel the world. Buy anything that caught his eye. He looked forward to that day, but it wasn't what drove him. Hitting the mother lode —*success*—was enough. And he was greedy for it.

He glanced over to the restaurant's entrance, grimacing when he made eye contact with Mr. Reeves. The man waved. And even though Thaddeus didn't respond in kind, Mr. Reeves headed in his direction.

Thaddeus groaned. No matter what the man said, no matter how much he offered, Thaddeus was done. He'd said as much after writing the last letter to the man's mail-order bride. And he'd meant it.

Mr. Reeves took off his hat as he approached Thaddeus' table. "Mr. Gray."

There was no way to avoid him, and the quickest way to get something over with was to do it and be done. "Mr. Reeves." He nodded slightly. "I thought we'd finished with our business."

The man's balding head bobbed. "We did. We *had*. But I need help."

Before he could continue, Thaddeus raised a hand and shook his head. "I'm sorry, Mr. Reeves, but I'm unable to help you further."

The man's eyes widened with panic. "You don't understand. She's coming! She'll be here on the afternoon train!"

Mr. Reeves had hired Thaddeus to write letters to his mail-order bride. He hadn't felt confident enough in his own penmanship—or intelligence—to write them himself. Normally, Thaddeus would never have done such a thing, but Mr. Reeves had paid him a hefty sum that had helped Thaddeus purchase new mining equipment without sacrificing anything else.

At first, writing to Miss Wigg had amused Thaddeus, intrigued him even, but after the second and final letter, when she'd spoken of her dreams for the future, his amusement fled and self-loathing burrowed in its place. It had seemed like a small lie to write to her as Mr. Reeves, before he'd realized what damage could be inflicted by doing so. She would never know of his deception, thankfully, but it still ate at him. "Congratulations. I'm sure you'll be very happy with Miss Wigg."

His felicitations were genuine, although he doubted Miss Wigg would be happy with Mr. Reeves. He seemed like a decent sort of person, and Thaddeus knew the man would treat her kindly. But a woman like Zara Wigg, a dreamer, would want more.

Thaddeus had recognized that in her. She was filled with passion about what mattered to her, and he doubted anything would stop her from achieving her goals.

He refocused on Mr. Reeves' aghast expression. "Is something amiss?" Thaddeus asked.

"Is something *amiss*? Of course it is! She's going to be here this afternoon. She doesn't know anything about me."

The man was barreling into a full panic. "Of course she does. I wrote as if I were you. You're a miner, you're holding out for the big strike. Was that not true?" *It also happens to be true about me.*

Mr. Reeves shuffled his feet. "Yes, but I don't sound so fancy in real life. All that talk about book learning..." He shook his head.

Thaddeus may have gotten carried away, he admitted. But her passion for Greek mythology, something he himself enjoyed, intrigued him. He'd read as many books on the subject as he could get his hands on, and it wasn't often he came in contact with someone so knowledgeable. She even spoke Greek. *Now that's dedication*, he thought admiringly. "All you have to do is be yourself. Speak with her. I'm sure she'll be reasonable, and you'll get along just fine."

"You think so?" There was a glimmer of hope in the man's tone.

"Absolutely. Without a doubt." Thaddeus glanced over the

man's shoulder to his approaching waiter. "Now, if you'll excuse me, my meal has arrived. Congratulations again."

Mr. Reeves nodded and turned away but didn't look completely confident. Thaddeus gave the man's intelligence a little more credit. If Thaddeus had someone write to his mail-order bride in his place, he'd be nervous as well. He just hoped Miss Wigg never found out the truth. Because from what he knew of her, she wouldn't take it easily. And that was one complication Thaddeus planned to avoid.

CHAPTER 2

The grief Zara felt during her tearful goodbyes with Vera Mae, Wendi, and Yetta back in Chicago dimmed as she stepped onto the train platform in Promise Creek, Montana. A gentle, mild breeze caressed her face, and she smiled, taking it as a good omen. It was as if the same breeze had been at each stop along her journey, gently pushing her West toward her destiny like her own personal zephyr.

Excitement pulsed through her as her gaze sifted through the male-dominated crowd, hoping to feel a connection with the man who would be her husband.

The logical part of her brain pressed that such things didn't happen. People didn't have soul mates. There wasn't any sort of spiritual recognition between two separate bodies. But she shushed that part of her brain. *This* would be different. This was going to be like every book she'd ever read, every fantasy she'd ever had, and every dream she'd ever dreamt. She just knew it.

Her life had been ordinary up 'til this point. *Boring.* Oh, she was grateful for everything Wiggie had done for her. Without her, Zara would've been on the streets. She never would have gained an education, never would have formed a family as she had, and she never would have had this opportunity to become a wife and open her own school.

But with the excitement pulsing through her, her nerves lighting on fire, she knew nothing would be the same again.

She sucked in a deep breath, inhaling pungent late summer smells. It was one of her favorite times of year. Children were excited to start up school after a long break, and fall was around the corner with its glorious colors and chilled air. Zara couldn't wait to snuggle up by the fire with her new husband as they talked late into the night—but first she had to find him.

As she scanned the platform once more, she saw a man with shaggy red-and-gray hair and matching beard. He looked at her earnestly, holding his hat in his hands—as if he were waiting for someone.

As if he were waiting for *her*.

Disappointment welled in her belly, and she forced herself to smile at him.

A wide grin spread across the man's face, softening his unkempt appearance. Zara could tell he was kind just by looking at him, but unfortunately, she didn't feel that instant attraction or thrill she'd hoped for.

She straightened her back, mentally berating herself. There was more to a person than their outward appearance. She knew that well. And it didn't matter what he looked like, he'd written her those beautiful, touching letters. She might not be outwardly attracted to him, but that didn't mean they wouldn't have a good marriage. Anyone who wrote letters like that was someone she was sure to fall in love with.

As he approached her, she smiled brightly. "Mr. Reeves?"

He nodded a bit too enthusiastically. "Miss Wigg!"

"It's a pleasure to meet you. I'm thrilled to finally be

here," she said, realizing that, even through her disappointment, she was.

"I'm glad you're here too." He glanced down at the small bag she'd carried off the train. "Here, let me get that for you."

She handed it over even though it hadn't been a burden. "Thank you." She glanced around the train station again, taking it all in. This place was her new home.

"Is the town as you expected?"

She returned her gaze to him. "Honestly? It's better." Some people might not be impressed by the small city when compared to the East, but Zara found it to her liking. Everything was clean and well maintained. The people here took pride in their homes, and she appreciated that.

"Well, good then. I was worried how you'd feel."

She chuckled. "This is a much better home than Persephone was presented with, I'm sure."

Mr. Reeves frowned. "Persephone?"

"Yes. Persephone...and Hades?"

He scratched his head. "Can't say I've ever heard of them."

"You've never heard of them?" It was her turn to sound dumbfounded. "But in your letter..."

His face cleared up, and he chuckled nervously. "Oh! From the letters. I remember now." He forced another laugh.

It was possible he'd forgotten, but something about the situation didn't feel right. "It's hard to forget when a mortal girl gets brought to heaven to become a servant to all the gods and goddesses," she said, testing him with incorrect information.

"That's true," he said uneasily. "Although I'm proud of Promise Creek, anyone might prefer heaven over it. Even if they were a servant. I remember you saying you enjoyed Greek history."

She forced a laugh as panic filled her. *This isn't right.* This was Mr. Reeves. He had to be. After all, it would be impossible to keep up such a charade in a small town like this one. Plus, he'd known her name, when she would arrive, and that she liked Greek history. He only could have known that if he'd read her letters.

He offered another smile. "Let's fetch your trunks and settle you at the hotel."

Worry ate at her, but she kept a straight face. "In your letter, you wrote about something that happened to you when you were young. Something that changed you. What was it?"

He shuffled his feet and looked away. "Oh, well, I wrote that so long ago I don't remember."

"You don't remember?" she asked slowly. "About something that changed your life?"

Panic flashed in his eyes, and he stumbled over his words. She remained silent, allowing him to unravel, as she had so many times with students at the orphanage. Finally, he broke.

"I'm sorry, Miss Wigg," he howled. "I swear, I only did it because I wanted to impress you."

"Did what?" She needed to know exactly what was going on.

"I had Mr. Gray write the letters for me. You see, he has more learning than I do, and I worried, after finding out you're a teacher, I wouldn't be quick enough for you."

She closed her eyes as her deepest fear unfolded. *He didn't write the letters.* "I don't know what to say. I'm shocked."

The man hung his head low. "I'm sorry I tried to trick you into marrying me. I was desperate. But what I did was wrong." He slumped. "You can't marry me."

She agreed wholeheartedly, but what would she do now? "I appreciate your honesty, Mr. Reeves. Although, I'm in a bit of a bind."

He shook his head. "I'm sorry I wasted your time, but I

have enough money to send you back. You can try again with someone else."

The thought of going back to the orphanage repelled her —she was ready to start a new life. Besides, all the others had left. "I'm not sure what I want to do."

"I understand. I've already paid for you to stay at the hotel for three days, and I'll cover all your expenses. Stay that time, then make up your mind. And either way, I swear to you, I will send you home if it's what you want."

All she could do was nod and agree. She had some money, but not much. It might get her a couple weeks in the hotel if she made it stretch, but not much else. Silently, he took her baggage ticket and retrieved her luggage. Nothing was turning out like she'd hoped.

What was she going to do now?

⚜

As soon as Mr. Reeves got her to the hotel and turned her over to the hotel staff, he hightailed it out. Zara shook her head as she watched her would-be husband's form retreat.

Of course she was upset about what he'd done, how dishonest he'd been with her. But more than anything, she pitied him. What sort of loneliness pushed a person to do such a thing? Zara had to believe there were other women who'd be happy to marry Mr. Reeves. After all, he was kind. Instead of lashing out when she'd uncovered his deceptions, he'd been penitent. Things could have gone very differently, and she was grateful she hadn't thought of the danger she'd put herself in by coming west all alone.

She should head back to the orphanage as soon as possible. What else could she do? Wiggie had made it abundantly clear she needed a husband—it was a condition for Zara to receive the funds for her school. And while she'd been more than happy to become a mail-order bride, she was leery now. What if she wrote another man who deceived her? What if that man was then unwilling to send her home? She'd be stuck.

Becoming a mail-order bride had seemed so glorious and grand. But Zara now realized it wasn't the fantasy she thought it'd be. Was there any way she could make the best of the situation and stay in Promise Creek? No matter what had happened, she still really liked the town. Everyone she'd spoken with, everything she'd seen, showed her it was a good place to settle down. And with so many men, it wouldn't take long to find a husband, would it? Would she even need to tell Wiggie?

She bit her lip as she contemplated how to handle the situation.

Someone cleared their throat behind her, and she swiveled around. A bellman nodded in greeting. "Your trunks have been delivered to your room. If you'd like, I can escort you there. Or, if you're hungry, I can take you to the dining room."

Part of her wanted to run to her room, lick her wounds, and figure out what to do. But she hadn't eaten all day, and she was starving. So as tired as she was, she said, "I'm famished."

The man smiled understandingly. "Right this way." He led her across the lobby toward a large entryway. There was a podium in the center, flanked on each side by lush potted plants. The maître d', an older gentleman dressed in a tuxedo, nodded regally to her, before giving his attention to the bellman.

"Miss Wigg will be dining alone this evening."

The maître d' nodded without judgment. "Please follow me, Miss Wigg."

The bellman smiled reassuringly at her before Zara followed the older man into the main dining area. He led her to a table in the middle of the room, and her shoulders eased as she noted the other single diners.

"Does this meet with your satisfaction?" he asked.

"It's wonderful," she said, truly meaning it as he assisted her into a chair. "Thank you."

A small smile lifted his lips. "Very good." He gestured for a server, and a man wearing a dress shirt and slacks, came to his side. "This is Mr. Springer. He'll be serving you this evening. If there's anything we can do for you, please don't hesitate to ask."

Zara had never been treated so well in her life. She'd worn her best dress to meet Mr. Reeves, a cerulean blue that complemented her dark brown hair and eyes. But besides the color, the embellishments were few. The cloth was the finest she'd been able to afford, but it wasn't anywhere near the quality wealthy women wore back home. Did they treat all women this way? "Thank you again."

As Mr. Springer listed all the specials along with several of the most liked dishes on the menu, her head whirled. Everything sounded incredible, but her exhaustion had caught up with her. She offered him an apologetic smile. "Everything sounds delicious. But after traveling for so long, I find it hard to make a choice. Which is your favorite?"

The man looked surprised as if no one had ever asked him such a thing. "My favorite dish?"

"Yes. At least, if you've tested items on the menu. I'm not sure how restaurants do things," she added, hoping to lessen any embarrassment she might have caused.

"I've tested everything, in fact." He straightened, as if proud. "Mr. Winthrop insists upon it. I've just never had anyone ask me that before."

Zara smiled. "Mr. Winthrop sounds like a very smart man. So? Which is your favorite?"

"Do you like beef?"

Her mouth practically watered. "Who doesn't?"

He laughed. "How about I surprise you. Do you have a budget?"

Mr. Reeves had said he would cover all expenses, including her meals. "No. Send me whatever your favorite is."

He gave her another flourishing bow before returning to the kitchens.

All alone again, she looked around the room, observing the other guests. Some were rushing through their meals like the place was on fire, while others savored, sipping their soup, relishing each taste. Normally, she rushed through her meals. There wasn't much time at the orphanage to dillydally. And on her trip here, there hadn't been much time between stops.

This was her first opportunity to slow down, to enjoy life. It was odd, really. She'd always dreamed of this moment, never fully believing she'd get here, but it was happening. She might not have a husband, but she was on her own, living her life. Even if that life was a bit of a mess.

How had everything gone wrong? The letters Mr. Reeves had sent to her—written by a Mr. Gray, apparently—had touched her. They'd spoken to her soul, and she'd known the person who wrote them was destined for her.

But it was all a lie. *Everything* was a lie.

She'd left her home, her friends, and now found herself alone in a strange new place.

And while she might have resented her circumstances, as she looked around, she realized...she liked it here. This was a place she could call home. And the fact was, Promise Creek still needed a school. Mr. Gray had told her the town was growing, that families were settling there, and their children would need an education.

And she still wanted that. But how? Without a husband, Wiggie would never agree to give her the funds she needed.

Looking around the room again, she noticed a large number of men, same as she had at the train station. And those men kept stealing glances at her. It wouldn't be hard to find another man to marry, would it?

And at least she'd have some time to get to know them. She wouldn't have to marry a *complete* stranger. Although, she didn't have the luxury of a long courtship either. And what would she do in the meantime? She only had three days at the hotel.

She sighed. Everything was such a mess.

She looked down, straightening the napkin in her lap, and when she looked up she saw a man walk into the room. She gasped as goosebumps raced along her skin. Her heart raced, knocking heavily against her ribs.

And when his eyes met hers—heat enveloped her.

He came to a stop as if unable to take another step. The maître d' continued on without him, oblivious of the man's reaction. But he just stood there, his eyes locked with hers.

She couldn't look away, and she didn't want to. Butterflies danced in her stomach, and her pulse raced. This man, whoever he was, was special.

This was what she'd been waiting for, what she thought she'd find when she stepped off the train.

As if realizing what he'd done, the man smiled at her, chagrined. He moved toward her, stopping a foot away from her table. She felt as if she were going to faint or do something else ridiculous.

His eyes roamed over her, taking in every detail. "Good evening," he said.

She cleared her throat. "Good evening."

"You're new, aren't you? I don't think I've seen you before."

"Yes. I arrived this afternoon." She couldn't look away from his deep blue eyes, now sparkling with even more interest.

"Will you be staying long?"

Her gaze darted away, and she hesitated. "I'm not certain."

"Is someone joining you?" He looked around as if another person would arrive at any moment.

She shook her head. "No. I'm dining alone tonight."

His eyes warmed. "I know this is forward, but may I join you?"

"You want to join me for dinner?" The question came out as a squeak.

His lips quirked. "Yes. I happen to be eating alone as well."

This can't be happening. It's too much. Like a fairytale she'd read from one of her books. But instead of allowing reality to crash in, she smiled and nodded, taking a leap of faith. "I'd like that."

Pleasure crossed his features, and it made her giddy. He looked over his shoulder to the maître d', who patiently waited at another table, and waved him over. "Yes, sir?"

"I apologize for the inconvenience, but it appears I'll be joining the lady for dinner."

To Zara's surprise, the maître d' looked at her for confirmation, and she nodded. She appreciated that she was given a chance to refuse.

"Did you order already?" he asked, sitting in the chair across from her.

"I did."

"What did you pick?"

"I didn't." Her lips curved. "Pick anything, that is," she explained at his confused look. "I didn't know what was good, so I asked my server to bring me his favorite."

"I guess it will be a surprise for both of us."

She was smiling in response when her waiter approached the table and looked at her dinner companion. "Your usual, sir?"

"Yes. Thank you."

And just like that, the server was off to the kitchen. She quirked a brow. "Your usual? How often do you eat here?"

He cleared his throat. "Every meal." He looked embarrassed.

"Why does that make you uncomfortable?" she asked, deciding to be forthright.

"Because I feel as though I should fend for myself more."

She laughed then. "If I could afford to eat in a place like this that often, I would. Don't get me wrong, I know how to cook, and I've had a lot of practice. But, for a while at least, it would be nice to have someone waiting on me."

He laid his napkin across his lap and leaned forward. "I didn't grow up with people waiting on me either. I keep waiting for it to become second nature, but it hasn't. I wonder if it ever will. I sure hope not." He winked.

She snorted and shook her head. "I would hope not. Did you grow up here, in Promise Creek?"

He took a sip of water. "No. I came here about two years ago. I have a mine," he added, as if that were obvious. Maybe it should be in a town like this.

"That's exciting."

He shrugged. "It sounds a lot more glamorous than it is. Really, it's dirty and a lot of hard work."

She leaned back with a small smile. "Ah. Well, Ponos would be proud then." She felt her cheeks redden. She found Greek mythology endlessly fascinating, but sometimes she forgot others didn't. "Ponos is the Greek god of—"

"Hard labor and toil," he added with a grin. "I know."

Her mouth fell open on a laugh. "How do you know that? *No one* knows that."

"Well," he drew out the word, "I happen to like Greek mythology."

It was almost as though he were teasing her, but he couldn't have known it was a passion of hers. "I do too. I came here to be a teacher, actually, and I fully intend on teaching my students the subject."

His smile faded. "A teacher?" He paused. "I'm sorry, did you say you arrived today?"

"Yes," she replied.

He went rigid in his chair and looked away. "Is something the matter?" she asked. But she knew there was. It was like the connection they'd had only moments before never existed. Had she said something to offend him?

He was about to respond when their waiter approached with their meals. He placed a thick cut of prime rib in front of her, potatoes and carrots garnishing the plate. "For you, Miss." Then he placed a large T-bone steak and peas in front of her companion. "And your usual, Mr. Gray."

The fork Zara had just picked up clattered to the table. "Mr. Gray?"

He nodded once, his jaw set. "It's nice to meet you, Miss Wigg."

Shock filled her as she froze, unable to look away from him. This was the man who'd written her the letters, the one who had colluded with Mr. Reeves to deceive her into coming out West?

At the sudden tension, the waiter looked worriedly between them. "Is there something I can help you with, Miss?"

Zara reeled, unsure of what to say. Finally, she looked at Mr. Gray. "Did you know it was me? This whole time?"

He shook his head vehemently. "No. Not until you told me you were a teacher."

There were so many things she wanted to say and do. She

wanted to tear him apart for his deception that had led to her arrival in town. But already some of the other restaurant patrons were looking at them curiously, and she couldn't afford to draw this kind of attention to herself. Especially if she decided to stay and open a school.

"Perhaps it might be best if I retire for the evening," he said, standing from his chair, and saving her from walking away or making a scene. He turned toward the waiter. "Would you mind having this sent up to my room?"

"Of course, sir." He left to accomplish the task, leaving Zara and Mr. Gray alone. Regret crossed his face, and he looked like he wanted to say something, but instead, he curled his hand into a fist and lightly tapped the top of the chair back. "It was nice to meet you, Miss Wigg."

Instead of spewing the reprimand he richly deserved, she pressed her lips together and nodded firmly.

He left without another word.

Fortunately, the others in the restaurant went back to their meals as if nothing had happened. And Zara wished she could do the same.

But as she sat there, stirring food around her plate, she couldn't deny that something *had* happened. The minute she'd seen Mr. Gray, it had seemed all her dreams of meeting her future husband had finally come true. Only, she wasn't destined to marry Mr. Gray. She refused to have anything to do with him.

How had her dreams gone so wrong?

CHAPTER 3

At daybreak, Thaddeus Gray rode out in a fury. He'd been lying awake in bed all night, thinking about Miss Wigg. The minute he'd laid eyes on her, it had woken something in him. Her big brown eyes and that glossy brown hair she'd pinned up with just a few tendrils kissing her neck had captivated him.

He'd never been so attracted to a woman at first sight. But it was more than that; he'd been drawn to her. And the minute he spoke with her, sat with her, he felt as if his life had changed forever. She'd intrigued him, provoked him, amused him, and when she'd spoken of Ponos, she'd impressed him. He'd never found that combination in a woman. He wasn't ready for a wife, but last night, he'd been sure he'd found the right woman.

Until he realized who she was.

Thinking of her shock, her anger—her disgust—he swore and dismounted in front of Mr. Reeves' small cabin. It was still early, but Thaddeus didn't care. He banged on the door, waited a moment, and then banged again when he didn't hear movement inside.

Finally, a groan sounded and floorboards squeaked under someone's weight. "There better be an emergency," Mr. Reeves said from inside.

When the man yanked the door open, his step faltered. "Mr. Gray? What are you doing here?" He looked past Thaddeus' shoulder.

Thaddeus didn't wait for an invitation as he brushed past the unkempt man. "We need to talk."

The man scratched his head and closed the door. "All right. About what?"

Thaddeus whipped around. "About what? What do you think? I ran into Miss Wigg last night in the hotel."

"All right. She's staying there for three days."

"And then what?"

Mr. Reeves shrugged. "And then she's going home. At least, I think so."

"What do you mean she's going home? I thought she was going to be your bride."

The man straightened. "She found out I didn't write the letters. Real quick too." He frowned. "I realized we wouldn't be a good fit. Especially not after I lied to her like that."

"But what about her school?" Even if she wasn't married, why would she abandon that? He knew it was important to her.

"I guess she doesn't much care." He held up his hands.

Thaddeus closed his eyes and took a deep breath, stifling the impulse to wrap his hands around the man's neck. Truly, he didn't want to beat the man, he just wanted information. "Well, what did she say?"

Mr. Reeves rocked back on his heels. "Not much. She wasn't happy, that's for sure."

What woman would be happy about being deceived? Frustration surged through him. When he wrote the letters, he hadn't realized the havoc it could cause. Because of what he'd done, she was stranded in town, without a husband or any source of living. Thaddeus was responsible for all that.

And it ate at him.

His first sight of her in the hotel had stunned him, electrified him. Their eyes had met, and he felt as if he'd known her always. He'd thought such things were hogwash, only fit for fairytales. But he couldn't deny his feelings or how he'd reacted to her.

It had felt so right, sitting with her, talking to her, getting to know her. But when she'd heard his name—Thaddeus grimaced at the memory. "You told her I wrote the letters, didn't you?"

"I didn't see no harm in it." He shrugged. "She already knew I didn't write them."

Thaddeus jerked his head away. Truly, it didn't matter. After finding out who she was, Thaddeus wouldn't have been able to keep the truth from her. Still, he could've told her about it on his own terms, explained why he'd done it and apologized. Perhaps, she might have understood, or at least forgiven him. That likely wouldn't happen now. "I'll need to speak with her," he said more to himself than anything, but Mr. Reeves answered.

"I guess if you feel you need to. Although, I'm not sure what you think you'll accomplish. You won't talk her into marrying me, will you?"

Thaddeus swallowed the acerbic words that leapt to his tongue. "No. I have no intention of talking Miss Wigg into anything."

Mr. Reeves nodded. "Good. Because I realize I need to find my own bride."

It was the smartest thing the man had ever said. "That would be wise." Thaddeus fidgeted with the hat in his hand. "Well, I found out all I needed to know. I'll leave you to your day."

Mr. Reeves looked like he wanted to say something else, but he closed his mouth and shook his head, closing the door after Thaddeus.

As he rode away, Thaddeus didn't know how the man was willing to sit and do nothing to help Miss Wigg. They'd both treated her poorly, and it was their responsibility to set it right. Thaddeus didn't think sending her home accomplished that.

☙❧

THE NEXT DAY LOOKED BLEAK FOR ZARA. SHE HAD NO IDEA what to do, where to go, or who to turn to. But one thing had become clear last night when she couldn't sleep: she needed to send Wiggie a message explaining what had happened. There was no way Zara could continue with the plan for the school without her knowing.

But as she walked to the telegraph office, Zara dragged her feet, trying to talk herself out of it. She didn't fear Wiggie's wrath. Once she knew the situation, Zara was sure her guardian would be sympathetic, but she would also insist upon Zara's immediate return.

As she walked on the boardwalk past the bank, several men tipped their hats in polite greeting. At first, she'd found the attention unsettling, but as the men kept their distance, greeting her from afar, her unease settled, and she'd been able to assess the town further.

She'd been in shock yesterday, after finding out she'd been duped. But today she took in the sweet, fresh air, the way everything looked clean and bright in the sun, and the way others interacted in the town. She knew a little bit about the place, its history as a mining settlement, but it had grown considerably since then. Children frolicked in pretty yards, squealing in delight, and she'd seen more than one of them skipping out of the mercantile, hands full of licorice.

This place was prosperous, and the people happy. Those things attracted Zara. They were ready for a school, ready for their children to receive an education, and Zara craved to fulfill that need, to share her knowledge and her love.

But she wasn't willing to do it with a lie.

Squaring her shoulders, she put her chin up and marched the rest the way to the telegraph office. She greeted the man at the desk warmly, and he quickly took her information and her message, assuring her it would be sent immediately. With any luck, Wiggie would reply the next day, and Zara informed the worker where he could find her when the response came.

Stepping out of the office, she took a deep breath and tilted her face toward the warm sunlight. If she had to leave, which she knew she would, she wanted to remember this place, to soak up every detail she could. The thought of leaving already left an ache in her heart.

Without anything else to do, she made her way back to the hotel. She hadn't unpacked and had no intention to. Not with so short a stay. But what else would she do with her time?

Her interest rekindled as she remembered the hotel had a library. Perhaps Mr. Winthrop would have a book on Greek history she hadn't read. At least *that* would be a positive. She snorted. Coming all this way, just to read a book—it was something the others at the foundling home might believe she'd do. In any case, it would make a good story.

"Miss Wigg?"

The masculine voice sent gooseflesh up her arms, and she turned to face the speaker, her back toward the hotel entrance. "Yes?" Even before she saw his face, she knew who it was.

Mr. Gray took another step toward her. "Miss Wigg, I was hoping I could have a moment of your time."

Zara folded her arms, unsettled. Just looking at him, the way he filled out his expensive gray suit, the way his blue eyes flashed, and his blond curls shimmered in the morning sun, made her ache. *And it shouldn't,* she firmly told herself. This man had deceived her. He wasn't someone she could trust.

She just wished her body would remember that. "I'm sorry, Mr. Gray, but we have nothing further to discuss."

He frowned. "I've spoken with Mr. Reeves, and he apprised me of the situation. That you'll be leaving in a few days."

Her chin jerked up. It bothered her that they'd discussed her, but she shouldn't have been surprised. They'd been colluding all along. "As I told you yesterday, I'm not certain what I'm going to do. And frankly, it's none of your business. Now, if you will excuse me."

She turned from him, but he reached out and gently stilled her. "Miss Wigg, I know you don't want to speak with me, but I'm afraid we have things to discuss. From what you wrote, you were intending to start a school here. Have you changed your mind?"

"It's complicated." She had no intention of explaining herself or her circumstances to this man.

"Please," he said, softly. "I know you have no reason to trust me, but believe me when I say all I want is to help you."

He held out his hands as if he had nothing to hide, and Zara wanted to believe him, but she remained firm. "Why? Haven't you already done enough?"

He nodded slowly. "I deserve that. What I did was despicable and dishonest. You don't know me, but if you did, you'd know that I strive to do what's right. Integrity is very important to me. When I wrote the first letter, I had no idea the repercussions of it. But when I got your second letter, when I got to know you a little more..." His voice softened. "I realized then what I had done. But it was too late. I just hope it's not too late now."

"What does that even mean?"

"It means I'm going to help you." He looked determined, his body rigid like he was prepared for battle.

"And what if I don't want your help?" She raised a brow, challenging him.

He shook his head regretfully. "I'm afraid I won't be able to accept that. You find yourself in this circumstance because of something I did. And I need to make that right."

Zara could tell no matter how much she fought, he would dig in. She threw up her hands. "Do I not have a say? Isn't this the same as what you've already done?"

"No." He seemed to reconsider his words, and his head dipped to the side, a self-depreciating smile curving his lips. "Well, maybe a little bit. But I won't feel right until this is settled."

Zara didn't know if she wanted to scream in frustration or laugh. The truth was, she did need help. She'd prefer it from another, but no one else had lined up for the job. Finally, she shook her head, and a soft chuckle escaped her lips. "All right. But I don't know what you can do."

Sensing victory, his shoulders loosened and his stance widened. "You don't have to leave, you know. This town truly does need a school."

The ache returned to Zara's heart. "I know. I can see that." She gazed over the street again, at the residents going about their day. "It's a lovely place."

He crossed his arms and leaned against one of the poles supporting the boardwalk's awning. "If you saw it two years ago, you wouldn't recognize it. It's changed drastically in that time."

Zara believed that—progress wasn't slow, especially out

West. "I probably wouldn't recognize it two years from now either."

His eyes warmed. "That's probably true."

And Zara wanted to be a part of that change. She wanted it more with every passing minute. "I wish I could stay."

"Why can't you?"

Suddenly exhausted from the last twenty-four hours, she shrugged. "I didn't write this in the letter, but having the money to start a school, hinged on my being married."

He stilled. "What does being married have to do with starting a school? Does it make you a better teacher?"

She laughed. "No. In all honesty, getting married will be a distraction. I'll have to split my time between my students and a husband. And taking care of the house." She rolled her eyes playfully.

"You don't want to get married?"

For a moment, it looked as though her answer mattered to him. "Even with the complication, I want to marry," she answered honestly. "I want a family of my own."

The momentary tension left his frame as though he liked her response, and her heartbeat quickened before she chastised herself. It shouldn't matter what Mr. Gray thought about her aspiration to marry. He would have no part in it.

"Let's go back to the part where you need to be married to start a school."

"Right." She rocked back on her heels. "The woman who runs the orphanage, Wiggie, gave me funds to start a school under the condition I marry first. She didn't want to worry about my safety, about me being alone in a town so far away from home. Well, me and three others. We're the youngest, and she's been a mother to us for as long as we can remember."

Understanding lit in his eyes, and he nodded. "I see. But surely she'd understand, under the circumstances."

Zara shook her head slowly. "You don't know Wiggie." She smiled ruefully. "I'm certain she'll insist on me returning home, to try and find another mail-order groom. She's very protective. And unfortunately, she doesn't have much longer to see me settled. She's dying."

"I'm sorry to hear that." He looked her over slowly. "But I can tell you're not pleased about trying again."

"After what happened here? Definitely not."

He winced. "Have you asked her about it?"

"I sent a telegram just a moment ago."

He nodded, and she could see his mind working quickly. "You'll probably have your answer tomorrow."

She nodded glumly. "That's my thought as well. I'll probably be on the train the next day. Besides, I don't have much in the way of funds to stay in the hotel past what Mr. Reeves provided. Maybe a week or two at most."

"I might be able to help with that."

She shook her head firmly. "No. I can't let you do that."

"Just hear me out." He held up a hand, as if asking for her patience. "I'm not saying I'll pay for your stay, but I can help you find a way to provide for yourself."

She narrowed her eyes suspiciously. "How?"

"Don't look as though I asked you to sell your soul." He laughed. "I'm just saying I might be able to find a few people looking for private tutors for their children."

She brightened up. It wasn't her dream exactly, but it might allow her to stay long enough to convince Wiggie. "You really think you can?"

"No promises, but I think so."

She chewed her lip, thinking it over. "If you can find someone, and they're willing to pay some of my wages in advance, I could stay at the hotel longer and try to get this figured out." Her excitement was coming back, and it bubbled to the surface as she looked at him. "I might be able to stay!"

His eyes warmed as he smiled at her. "I give you my promise that if you want to stay, I'll find a way for it to happen."

His declaration tied her stomach in knots. "You might come to regret that, Mr. Gray."

CHAPTER 4

Thaddeus didn't consider this stalking. He stood outside the telegraph office, waiting to see if any telegrams came in—so he could then follow the messenger back to Miss Wigg.

He cursed, turned around and walked two steps away before turning back and resuming his vigil. He wished he had good news for her, but frankly, his search for someone looking for a tutor had come up short yesterday. Apparently, he didn't know many people with families. The only men he was acquainted with were rough miners like himself. He rolled his eyes, realizing how truly pathetic that was. But he refused to give up. He'd continue looking.

He hoped her guardian would have better news. Surely the woman wouldn't penalize Miss Wigg for her mail-order groom's deception. Regardless of what Miss Wigg thought, it just wasn't rational.

He checked his timepiece for the hundredth time that morning, wondering how much longer he'd have to wait. Sure, he had other things to do, but he couldn't focus on them. Not when he had to set this right. With any luck, the telegram from Wiggie would fix the problem.

He'd just leaned against the building when the door to the telegraph office opened, and the worker quickly made his way out. Thaddeus straightened and moved into action.

He trailed the man and didn't bother hiding it as they strode to the hotel. As he stepped into the entrance, he heard the man ask for Miss Wigg.

This is it.

The clerk summoned another employee, and the man disappeared into the hotel, no doubt tracking down Miss Wigg.

Thaddeus knew he cared about what happened to Miss Wigg, but he hadn't realized the extent of his interest. He felt tense with suspense. And when Miss Wigg entered the room, following the hotel employee, Thaddeus' body tightened further.

He didn't know how it was possible, but she was even more attractive today than yesterday. Her hair and clothes were simple and yet utterly flattering. Truly, as he gazed at her, he couldn't think of another woman who'd entranced him so.

But it wasn't just the way she looked. Since speaking with her, he hadn't been able to get her off his mind. He wanted to know everything about her, every detail of her past, her secrets, and what made her, *her*.

He rubbed the back of his neck, suddenly worried about what that meant. If he was only physically attracted to her, it would've been easy. He'd been attracted to many women in his life. But this was different. She fascinated him, beguiled him.

He was in trouble.

But instead of worrying over that fact, he felt almost

amused. He'd been obsessive with his mine since coming to town. Perhaps he might feel differently toward her if he didn't have a hunch he was close to his big break, that he was about to live the rest of his life outside the dark tunnels in the mountain. He didn't want to be alone, that was for certain. And maybe, just maybe, he was opening to the possibility of marriage.

Miss Wigg might not be the woman for him—she'd made it clear she wasn't interested—but perhaps he should think about finding someone soon. Someone who cared for him *before* he made his fortune.

He shook the fanciful thoughts out of his head as he stepped toward Miss Wigg. Before he could think about any of that, he needed to make sure she was taken care of.

Her velvety brown eyes met his in confusion. "Mr. Gray? You wanted to see me?"

He shook his head, but before he could say anything else, the telegraph operator stepped forward. "Miss Zara Wigg?"

His attention caught on her Christian name, and he had the sudden urge to say it out loud. He'd seen it in the letters of course, but the sound of it stuck in his mind. It suited her perfectly.

Zara nodded. "I am she."

Without wasting another moment, the man handed her a telegram. "This just came in for you. I can wait if you'd like to reply."

Zara looked at the telegram, no doubt seeing her guardian's name, and shook her head. "That won't be necessary. Thank you, though. I'll come in if I need to reply."

The man tipped his hat. "Very good," he said, before heading out of the hotel.

Zara blew out a heavy breath as she looked at the paper.

Thaddeus stepped closer. "Is something wrong?" he asked softly.

She shook her head but smiled ruefully. "I don't think I've ever been so afraid to read a message in my life."

He understood completely. The few lines on the paper would determine her future. *He* was on edge, and it had nothing to do with his life. He couldn't even imagine how she felt. "Do you want me to read it?"

"No. I can do this."

But before she could open it, he took her arm and led her to the side of the room. He wanted to be out of the main thoroughfare in case Zara reacted poorly.

As if knowing why he'd done it, she smiled and then turned her attention back to the telegram. "My hands are shaking."

"Read it quickly and get it over with."

She nodded and opened the paper, her eyes scanning it quickly. She seemed to read it a second time before she folded the paper again, her shoulders deflating.

He frowned. "Is it bad?"

She shrugged. "Not as bad as expected, but worse than I'd hoped." She held up the paper for him. "You can read it, if you'd like."

He didn't hesitate. He took the telegram from her fingers and scanned it quickly. Words momentarily left him. Finally, he looked up at her. "She can't mean that."

"Oh, she most certainly does."

He was flabbergasted. "She's giving you two weeks to find a husband or else you need to return home? Who finds a husband in two weeks?"

"It's not ideal, I'll give you that. After what happened last time, I'm not keen on choosing someone quickly. I was foolish before." She shook her head regretfully. "I thought it would all work out. I thought it was like some grand love story. How wrong I was." She laughed humorlessly.

He hated seeing her like that. "It's possible to find someone in that time."

"Possible? Yes. But I'm not certain I should." She looked toward the door as if seeing outside. "I thought this was worth it. Finding a husband, coming here, starting a school. And it was—is. I do want to teach. I want to make children's lives better, to help them see they are capable of anything. But is it worth it at the expense of my future?" Her brows furrowed, and she looked lost. "I don't know anymore."

Protectiveness filled him. "I know you can find someone who will be a good husband. And you can do it in that time. I'll help you."

Surprise filled her eyes as her gaze locked with his. "You're going to help me find a husband?"

"Yes."

As if remembering his earlier promise to help her, she asked, "Were you able to find anyone for me to tutor?"

He could hear the hope in her voice, and it gutted him. "No. Not yet anyway. With the town growing, many people feel it's only a matter of time until a school is started. Most want to wait until that happens."

He shook his head at the irony, but Zara seemed to understand. "Thank you for trying."

"I'm not finished looking."

She shook her head slowly. "This feels so pointless. No one wants to hire me as a tutor, but I can't start a school until I have a husband. But it seems like an impossible task to meet someone, get to know them, and then marry all within two weeks." Her shoulders sagged. "Maybe I should just go home."

Her words lit something in him. The thought of her leaving, of never seeing her again, shook him. But instead of saying so, he lashed out. "Are you really going to give up so easily?"

Her eyes widened in disbelief. "Give up? I think it's pretty obvious I've been defeated."

"Hardly. You haven't even started. There are so many men in this town who would gladly marry you *today*." It was the truth, but the thought made him uncomfortable. It didn't stop him from continuing though. "You'll have your pick. Really, the only thing stopping you from starting your school is yourself."

Her spine straightened so quickly he wondered if she'd hurt herself, and she tapped his chest with her index finger. "I'm not stopping myself from reaching my dreams. I'm here, aren't I? I traveled across the country, left my home and family, and I'm still here."

Her spirit took his breath away. When angry, she lit up, her face flushed, and he could see the passion simmering in her eyes. It made him wonder how she'd react if he kissed her. But instead of following through with that desire, he banked it. "You *are* here. Now there's just one more thing to do."

"Finding someone isn't that simple."

He smiled. "How hard can it be?"

THADDEUS HADN'T KNOWN HOW WRONG HE WAS ABOUT finding her a husband.

Someone had overheard their conversation in the hotel, and news of Zara's need for a husband spread through the town like wildfire. The number of men vying for her hand had gotten so out of control that she hadn't been able to leave the hotel on her own.

When the thought had occurred to him to help her find a husband, he'd imagined a much more manageable experience. But this? It was utter chaos.

He walked into the hotel foyer, weaving through the groups of men already there, waiting for a glimpse of Zara.

It was even worse than it had been last night when the news broke, and Thaddeus wondered how large the crowd would be by day's end.

He shook his head. He needed to do something about it. But what?

He'd thought he would be able to head to the mine today while Zara adjusted to this new change, but it didn't look as though it would be possible.

"What on earth is going on?" An annoyed male voice came from behind him.

Thaddeus turned and saw Rhys Winthrop, the owner of the hotel, glaring at the crowd in the lobby. When no one answered him, Thaddeus approached him with a nod. "I apologize for the inconvenience, I didn't realize this was going to happen."

Rhys nodded in greeting. "Thaddeus. You're the reason they're here?"

In a roundabout way he was, but instead of explaining everything, he said, "No. They're here for Miss Wigg."

"Miss Wigg." He said the name, as if trying to put a face with it, then finally nodded. "Ah. Yes." He frowned, obviously piecing together what was happening. He raised his voice and spoke to the room. "Gentlemen, thank you for joining us this morning. If you're here for a room or meal, please speak with one of the employees promptly. Otherwise, you'll have to wait outside the establishment for Miss Wigg. Unless of course, one of you has an appointment already scheduled with her."

Thaddeus snorted. None of them had an appointment with her, of that he was certain. In fact, he pulled out his watch to check the time, he was supposed to meet with her in five minutes in the dining room for breakfast. He snapped the watch closed and tucked it back into his vest. With any luck, the crowd would be gone by the time she came downstairs.

Grumbles sounded, but the men began exiting the building, and after a few minutes, the almost deafening noise from earlier was down to the normal murmur of the lobby.

He hadn't thought it'd be possible, but before Zara descended the stairs, each of the men had left, thanks to Mr. Winthrop's excellent staff.

She smiled at him from across the lobby, tucking a stray strand of silky brown hair behind her ear, almost self-consciously. But that didn't match up with what he knew about her. She was strong, resilient, and happy with who she was. He liked who she was too.

She stepped up to him and smiled. "Didn't we say we'd meet in the dining room?" A chuckle escaped his lips, and she raised an eyebrow. "Did I miss something?"

He nodded, and he could feel his eyes crinkle with amusement. "You did."

She glanced around the room, but clearly didn't see anything out of the ordinary. "What happened?"

"There were about fifty men crammed in here five minutes ago."

Her brows furrowed. "Fifty? Why..." Her jaw dropped. "You mean they were here for me?"

He nodded, stifling his amusement. Instead of being pleased with the attention, she appeared horrified. "As I said, you'll have your choice."

"But they don't even know who I am! They don't know anything about me."

He shrugged. "You're a woman."

She huffed. "I'm not sure I like the thought of someone marrying me just because I'm a woman. How unflattering."

He could see her point. "I'm sure we'll come up with

something. Let's go into the dining room and talk over your options."

She nodded reluctantly but followed him. He was just about to ask for a table when three men converged on them.

"Miss Wigg! It's lovely to see you."

"Miss Wigg, will you have breakfast with me?"

"Miss Wigg, I have something to ask you—"

Zara's eyes widened as men continued to bombard her with attention faster than she could respond, and a tidal wave of protective fury filled him. He stepped closer and wrapped an arm around her before pulling her snuggly against him. "Step away from her, now."

She leaned against him as if trying to hide. And while a thrill coursed through him as she sought safety in his arms, he was furious she was so uncomfortable. "You heard Mr. Winthrop earlier. If you'd like to talk to Miss Wigg, you'll have to wait outside the hotel." He nodded to the hotel workers who saw what was happening, and they immediately stepped forward to escort the men out.

When they were alone again, he lowered his arm, but Zara didn't move away. "Everything's all right." He reassured her. "I'm sorry that happened."

She shook her head. "I'm not sure *why* it's happening. I understand there's a shortage of women, but why don't these men send for their own mail-order brides?"

He dipped his head slightly. "Unfortunately, there aren't many women willing to make the trek out West. Especially to marry a man they've never met."

"I understand—it wasn't my first choice either." She looked at the dining room uneasily.

He followed her gaze and saw that several men in the room were watching her. He cursed. "Why don't I have the kitchen pack us a basket? We can take a drive."

She turned to him, her eyes wide. "Truly? Are you sure you have time?"

He'd wanted to get to the mine, but she was his current priority. "It'll be fine. It's one of the perks of working for myself."

She chuckled, and he could see her body relax at the thought of getting away. "That's definitely a positive."

He smiled at her. "Why don't you wait in the private dining room while I get everything ready? I'm sure that won't be a problem, considering the circumstances. I'll come get you when it's time."

He was about to turn away when she reached out and placed a hand on his forearm. He glanced down at her delicate fingers before looking up to her eyes.

"Thank you," she said softly. "I'm not sure how I'd handle all this without you."

"*Without me*, you wouldn't be in this situation." He wasn't going to let her forget it. Because when she looked at him like that, with warmth and trust, it made him forget they shouldn't be together.

"That's true. But Mr. Reeves would've had someone else write the letter if you'd refused, and I sincerely doubt that person would be helping me as you are."

He couldn't disagree, so he nodded briskly. "Go on now. I'll find you in a moment."

She nodded, and her hand slipped from his arm as she left. Although she no longer touched him, she'd left a mark on his heart. And he wondered if it would ever go away.

CHAPTER 5

When Thaddeus stepped into the private dining room, his face grim, Zara knew something was wrong. "What happened?" She could see he tried to calm his expression, but it didn't matter. She read the frustration in his eyes, the rigidness of his posture.

"We might have a problem."

"We couldn't get a picnic basket?" she asked, hoping such a minor thing was the problem.

He looked at her in chagrin, but then shook his head and smiled. "I only wish the picnic basket was the problem." She twisted her fingers in front of her as she waited for him to continue. "As I was hitching the wagon, I noticed the crowd in the front of the building. I hoped the men would disperse, but it appears as though they're waiting until you come out."

"How many?" Her voice was faint.

"Fifty? Seventy-five? I'm not certain."

Her stomach dropped. There were that many men waiting outside for her? "What can we do?"

"From now on, we'll be more discreet, but they already

saw me hitching up the wagon and know you're coming with me. We'll have to head out the front."

"There's no way to slip out the back?"

He shook his head and stepped forward, taking her hand and squeezing it. "No. Not this time. In the future we'll take more precautions, but you're going to have to walk through the crowd today."

She swallowed hard. This had all sounded so grand before, like she was a princess who knights fought over. Now she realized it was just chaos. She was intimidated and wasn't going to pretend otherwise, but instead of cowering, she lifted her chin. "You'll be with me?"

He squeezed her hand again, and the warmth of his palm steadied her. "The entire time. Also, I spoke with Mr. Winthrop, and his employees will help keep the crowd back."

She nodded in acceptance. There wasn't much else to do. "Let's go, then."

"Stay right behind me. I'll cut a path," he said as he led her out of the room.

As if she'd do anything else. She followed him, slightly relieved when she saw the hotel employees waiting for them at the entrance. "Are you ready?" one of them asked, and Thaddeus nodded.

They opened the doors, and Thaddeus didn't waste any time before stepping out. She followed close behind, but when she saw the sheer number of men waiting for her, their cheers sounding in the air, she froze.

In those few seconds of shock, Thaddeus had moved several steps ahead of her, leaving a gap between them that quickly filled in.

Men were introducing themselves so quickly she couldn't keep track, and their voices filled her head like bees.

"Why don't you take a drive with me, Miss Wigg, instead of him?"

For some reason, that particular question stood out to her, and she looked up at the man who'd spoken. "I apologize, but not this time. Perhaps another?"

The man with light brown hair grinned and crowed to the crowd, "You hear that, fellas? She said yes to me!"

Someone else yelled, "She'll say yes to me too!"

A retort sounded, and then one man pushed another, followed by a swift shove back. Someone grabbed her skirt, shocking her. She tugged the material and stepped backwards into the chest of another man.

But before she could even squeak, she was pulled forward and encased in arms of iron. She went rigid until Thaddeus' familiar scent filled her nose. "Step back!" he roared.

She could feel anger radiating from him, but she didn't care. She was grateful he was protecting her. He quickly guided her to the wagon and lifted her up to safety. Instead of rounding the vehicle, he climbed up after her and squeezed past her, quickly setting the horses into motion.

Men jumped out of the way to avoid the horses' hooves. Perhaps they knew Thaddeus wouldn't stop.

As they quickly left town, she shivered, reeling from what had happened.

"Are you all right?"

She didn't answer.

"Are you all right, Zara?"

Hearing him use her Christian name jolted her. "I'm fine."

He cursed under his breath. "I'm sorry this is happening to you. I wish I could stop it."

She heard the anguish in his voice, the self-loathing. He blamed himself for this, but she didn't. "I imagine it would happen to any single woman."

He laughed harshly. "You have no idea. We've had groups of women coming into town recently, and the men have lost their minds."

She shivered. She could just imagine. "At first, I thought it would be nice to pick my own husband. But now..." She shook her head, remembering the mob outside the hotel. "Now I just wish the whole thing was over."

He nodded grimly but didn't speak again. They rode in silence for another ten minutes before he pulled off the road to a lesser used trail.

She frowned. "Where are we going?"

"Somewhere safe."

"Well, that's reassuringly vague."

He gave her a side smile before focusing back on driving. "I'm taking you to my claim. It's safe there, and no one knows where it is."

Her interest was piqued. "I've never seen a mine."

He laughed. "Don't sound so excited. It isn't much to look at."

She rolled her eyes. "Well, I didn't imagine it was Zeus' palace or anything."

"The complete opposite, in fact."

"All right, so you aren't Plutus."

He grinned at her. "*Yet*."

The rest of her anxiety from the men's attentions faded. "If you become like the god of wealth, you'd have enough to build Zeus' palace one hundred times over."

"And that's exactly what I intend. To build Zeus' palace one hundred times over," he teased.

She gently pushed his arm. "Bragger."

"Just sharing a bit about my wishes and dreams."

She raised a brow. "And you dream of having one hundred palaces?"

"I dream of being able to buy or do anything I want for the rest of my life."

His voice had turned serious, and she studied him. "Why do you want that?"

"Who wouldn't? Don't you?" He gave her a quick glance before turning onto another path which forked at a large, gnarled tree.

She frowned, thinking about it. "It would be nice to have whatever I wanted. Although..." She cocked her head. "It would make life boring. I can't say it's something I ever dreamed about. Maybe because it seems so impossible."

He nodded in understanding. "Something you come to understand after being out here for a while is that nothing is impossible in the West. You can re-create yourself, build a fortune, become anything you want. That's what's so great about being here. There aren't any rules, and you aren't held back by anything." He shrugged. "Nothing will hold you back but yourself," he amended.

She liked the thought of that. Anything she hoped for, anything she dreamed of, could happen. It was how she'd always imagined her life would be, when she'd been in the orphanage, but the past few days had taught her that reality was far from her dreams.

Thick foliage brushed up against the cart, and Thaddeus swatted at a branch. "Not much farther."

Regardless of what he'd said, she was excited to see it. And just then, the mine came into view. "Hmm."

He laughed as he stopped the horses. "I told you."

He'd been right. There was an unimpressive opening in the mountain, secured by coarse, wooden beams. The plants had been cleared away, and the ground was barren, except for an assortment of tools scattered around. The cracked, compacted dirt made a sturdy, if unimpressive, floor. "It's, um, lovely."

His eyes twinkled in amusement as he hopped down, rounded the cart, and reached up for her. She was so busy looking in his eyes, she hadn't prepared herself for his touch.

But as he wrapped his arms around her waist, her breath froze in her lungs.

The other times he'd touched her, tucked her against his body, had been moments of distress. And the distractions had dampened the potency. But there was nothing distracting her now. His touch sent a wave of longing through her.

He hesitated before placing her down, but it was enough to tell her he felt the same connection.

He stepped away quickly, reaching into the wagon for the basket. "Where would you like to set up?"

Hoping to calm herself, she glanced around, finally spotting a small section of grass. "I think that sad little patch is our only option."

He snorted in amusement, and she was grateful she'd eased the tension between them. He moved over to where she'd pointed, opened the blanket, and spread it over the ground. When he knelt down, she followed suit and made sure to sit on the opposite side of the blanket. "Are you hungry?" he asked.

"Ravenous, actually." She didn't bother hiding it. Eating was a necessity of life. She didn't understand why some women pretended they didn't eat.

He tossed her a smile. "Good. Because there's enough to feed an army."

He pulled out cold cuts of meat, fruit, and an assortment of pastries. Her eyes widened. "You weren't kidding." There was plenty of food, but with how hungry she was, and with the stress of earlier, she was sure they'd eat through it. "Would you like me to fix the plates?" she offered.

He shook his head and waved her away. "No, I'll take care of it. You sit and relax."

She did as he asked, but it surprised her. She hadn't courted much, but in her experience, women normally handled such things. The fact he was willing, and had even insisted upon doing it, filled her with pleasure. Thaddeus wasn't like anyone she'd met in the past. Was it because he was a man of the West? If she'd gotten to know any of the other men in town, would she find the same characteristics?

The thought intrigued her, but she doubted it was true. From what she'd seen, the men around town were very much like men back East. "Thank you."

"Is there anything you don't like?"

She eyed the spread again. "Everything looks heavenly."

His grin turned mischievous. "Then I'll make sure to put a lot of it on your plate."

A surprised laugh escaped her when he did just that. "You'll make it so my dresses no longer fit."

"You've uncovered my devious plan. But your husband will be able to afford the expense of a new wardrobe."

She knew he was teasing, but the comment brought back her worry. She bit her lip. "*If* I find a husband."

His hands slowed in their mission of piling food as high as a skyscraper on her plate. He cleared his throat. "There's something I'd like to talk to you about."

She wasn't sure what else there was to say. Especially not after the madness of earlier. "Oh?" He handed her the plate, and she blindly put a pastry in her mouth, hardly tasting the sugary flavor.

"Yes. I think it would be best if your suitors were hand-picked for you."

Zara thought it over. "That would be ideal, but I'm not sure how it could be done." She cocked her head to the side, thinking it over. "While perhaps some of the men are literate, I assume not all are. If they were, I could have them fill out a questionnaire."

Thaddeus nodded. "That's a possibility. Although, as you said, not all can read and write." He frowned. "Is that something that will bother you? If your husband is illiterate?"

Zara shrugged, uncertain of the answer. "I don't know. I'd like to think it wouldn't. I wouldn't mind teaching my husband those things, although I'm not certain how he would feel about his wife teaching him."

"Any man that has a problem with it isn't worth your time."

His defense of her filled her belly with butterflies. "In any case, it would probably be nice to have someone who could read. We'd have more things in common."

His eyes met hers. "Yes. Then you could both discuss Greek mythology to your hearts' content."

She chuckled just imagining it. "If my husband can drone on and on about Zeus and Hera, Athena, Aries, or Poseidon, I'll be very well pleased."

"So you don't require him to speak Greek?"

She chuckled softly and shook her head. "I think that would be asking a bit much."

"I'll see what I can find." He paused. "You deserve only the best, Miss Wigg."

His words were spoken softly, and her eyes were drawn back to him. "You should call me Zara. In truth, I've been using your Christian name in my mind. Seems only fair."

"Zara," he agreed.

Hearing her name in his rich baritone again, caused gooseflesh to rise. "May I call you Thaddeus?"

"I'd like that." His voice turned deeper.

Desire swept through her, and, uncertain what to do, she reached for a container of lemonade. He reached for it as well, and his hand covered hers over the metal container. He didn't pull away. Instead, he left it there, and she absorbed the warmth from his skin. "Let me do it for you," he said softly.

Her mouth went dry, and she swallowed a few times before answering. "Are you going to let me do anything for you?"

His eyes dipped to her lips and lingered. Her skin tingled as if she could already feel him there. "You're letting me serve you. That's more than enough."

She wanted to lean forward and kiss him, to channel the scorching heat inside and share it, but she remained still, afraid of how he'd react.

Slowly, she leaned back, and her hand slipped out from under his. He didn't say anything else as he opened the lemonade and poured it into two separate glasses.

"Thank you," she said, as he handed her the beverage. She took a sip of the tart drink, and it made her mouth water.

He watched her with heated eyes, but he finally cleared his throat and looked away. "Zara…"

Her heart raced. It sounded like he had something important to say. "Yes?"

"I…" He cursed softly then looked at her. "It's about finding you a husband."

"Oh." Her shoulders deflated. She'd been certain, or at least she'd hoped, that he would say something else. For a moment, she'd wondered if he had feelings for her. Now she just felt foolish. Not wanting him to realize what she'd thought, she smiled brightly.

"Instead of writing a questionnaire, I could find you matches."

Her heart sunk. He wanted to find her a husband. It wasn't anything different than what he'd been doing before—helping her—but for a moment, she'd hoped he would put himself forward for that position. "I'm not sure."

He held up a hand. "Hear me out. Any time men get around you, they lose their heads."

Not you, she wanted to say. She'd been so angry when she'd first met him—well, that wasn't quite true. When she hadn't known who he was, she'd felt a connection with him, had wanted to get to know him, from the moment she saw him.

He continued talking, drawing her attention back. "But if I talk to the men first, I could find someone who would suit you."

She wasn't sure what to say. She wanted to vocalize her growing feelings for him, but she didn't think they'd be welcome. So instead, she cleared her throat. "All right. If you think it would be helpful."

"I do." He looked at her again, the warmth back in his eyes. "And more importantly, I think it will keep you safe."

She swallowed hard, wishing he would say more. Wishing, he would put himself forward to be her husband. "Then that's what we'll do."

CHAPTER 6

As Zara waited in Sally's cafe for one of the men Thaddeus had chosen, she swore they were the longest minutes of her life. Her nerves were already stretched thin, and the wait wasn't helping.

She glanced at the cafe's sparse late lunch crowd. It was the first time she'd eaten here, choosing to take her meals in the security of the hotel before now. The atmosphere, the charm of the place, appealed to her. Even though the town was full of men, Sally's had a homey touch that only a woman could achieve.

Every day that went by, Zara was getting more and more attached to Promise Creek. It was a place she could settle into, somewhere she could do some good—somewhere she'd be happy.

She let out a sigh, purposefully unlinking her fingers beneath the table. *There's no need to be nervous,* she reminded herself. She was here to *meet* the man. She didn't have to do anything else. This person was only one of her options, but she wondered what had prompted Thaddeus to pick him first.

At least she wouldn't have to wait much longer to find out.

She wanted to be hopeful and excited, but those emotions were proving elusive. The situation was too dire for that. Time was running out, and the only man she was interested in thus far, appeared to have no interest in her.

She sighed.

If only she had more time to find the right man, to be sure of herself and who she was choosing.

She shook her head. She needed to stop overthinking this. Zara was lucky Wiggie had given her the two weeks she had. Her guardian could have forced her to return home immediately to start searching again in a safer setting.

She was even more fortunate Thaddeus was helping her. If she were on her own, she wasn't sure how she would have managed the mob that had descended on the hotel.

Was it wrong she wished the whole thing was over with already? She was tired of the uncertain future, of unfulfilled plans and dreams. She wanted things settled so she could move on with her life.

And all of that started with finding a husband.

The cafe's door opened, and Zara straightened in her chair, hoping to make a good first impression. Instead of a stranger, her eyes met Thaddeus'. He smiled broadly at her as if truly pleased to see her, and her body flushed in pleasure. She couldn't help it. The more she was around him, the more attractive he became. It was exhilarating and frustrating and inconvenient, but no matter how she tried, she couldn't force her feelings away. Everything would be so much simpler without this toe-curling desire simmering through her.

Well, at least her date had been canceled. She relaxed in her chair, grateful for the reprieve—and then another man entered the restaurant. His neck was thick, straining against a tie that almost choked him. His torso was a tad too long for his legs, but he walked tall and proud, and Zara could tell the man was successful. He wasn't unattractive, exactly, but he wasn't the kind to catch a woman's eye either. But Zara brushed that off. Appearances weren't everything, she told herself, just as she had when she first met Mr. Reeves.

He glanced around the room, and she almost dismissed him—then his eyes landed on her. She straightened in her chair as he said something to Thaddeus.

This was one of the men Thaddeus had chosen to court her. Dread settled in her belly, and she wondered where the feeling came from.

Without wasting any more time, Thaddeus moved closer, nodding warmly to her in greeting. "Good afternoon, Miss Wigg. May I present Mr. Chesley. Mr. Chesley, Miss Wigg."

Zara smiled, hoping it looked friendly instead of as strained as it felt. Was she supposed to shake his hand? When he only offered a brisk nod by way of greeting, she was grateful she hadn't done more.

Thaddeus put his hands together, and she wondered if he felt the same awkwardness she did, "Well, now that you've been introduced, I hope you'll have an enjoyable lunch." He turned his attention to Zara, his eyes lingering on her a moment too long. "I'll be waiting to speak with you once you've finished."

She was grateful he'd said so in front of Mr. Chesley. It gave her a sense of protection, which calmed her. "I'll see you soon."

She watched him as he walked out the door. Disappointment filled her, but she mentally shook it off and gave Mr. Chesley her full attention. She hoped he hadn't noticed the way she watched Thaddeus leave. "I hope you're hungry." She offered him a bright smile.

He grunted in return. "Hungry enough. Sally's food is

tolerable." He eyed her then, and a sinking feeling settled in her gut. "I hope your cooking is better than hers."

Her eyes widened. "I beg your pardon?"

The man leaned back. "I won't have a wife who can't cook."

She reeled at his words, at the implication. It was as if she were interviewing to be his wife. In a way, she was, but his rudeness was intolerable. He acted as though she'd already agreed to marry him. "Forgive me, but I think you've misunderstood the purpose of this meeting."

"No, I understand just fine. You need a husband. I need a wife. But just because *you're* desperate, doesn't mean *I* am. I could get me one of those mail-order brides, make sure beforehand she can cook, is neat as a pin, and mighty fine looking." His eyes raked over her, and her skin crawled. "I prefer women with lighter coloring, but you're easy enough on the eyes."

Her mouth fell open, but nothing came out. All her retorts were trapped in her throat. She needed a husband, but she'd be loath to settle down with such a person. She didn't expect to be in love before she wed, but she demanded respect. And it was clear Mr. Chesley held no respect for her.

A woman she assumed was Sally walked over to their table, but before she could speak, Zara held up a hand and stopped her. "Forgive me. There's been a misunderstanding." She looked up at the gently aging woman. "I'm afraid I'm unable to stay for a meal just now. Excuse me," she said as she pushed away from the table.

Mr. Chesley blustered. "Where do you think you're going? We're not finished discussing our union."

She looked over her shoulder. "I should think it's obvious where I'm going. I'm leaving. I've decided you and I will not be a good fit. Good day."

Zara looked away from the man's reddening face to Sally's

amused eyes. "I'm sorry for the trouble," she said, apologizing once more.

Sally rocked back on her heeled boots and shook her head. "That's all right. I hope to see you again real soon."

Zara nodded and didn't waste another moment on Mr. Chesley before making her way to the door. The moment she stepped out of the cafe, she let her frustration out. "The nerve of that man!"

"Zara?"

Surprised, she whirled around, and Thaddeus straightened away from the building's exterior. "Zara, is everything all right?"

The concern in his eyes calmed her, but then she remembered *he* was the one who had found Mr. Chesley for her.

She pointed a finger at him. "I should fire you from finding me a husband if that's who you came up with."

His look went from concern to chagrin. "I take it you two weren't a match?"

"Not a match? I've never seen anyone so far from my ideal in my life."

He snorted. "Believe me, there are plenty of men much more objectionable than Mr. Chesley."

She folded her arms. "So, you're telling me it's hopeless? I'm never going to find a husband, and I should just return home?"

His teasing ceased. "Of course not," he said more softly. "I'm sorry. I shouldn't make light of the situation. He's not the only person I have in mind. I've found a few others, but he was by far the wealthiest and could take care of you the way you deserve."

She shook her head in disbelief. "I need more than money to make me happy. I appreciate you trying to put me in the best situation, but it'll only work if the man is a good fit for me. I need someone kind, someone who will treat me with respect." She looked at him doubtfully. "I just hope the others are better candidates. If not, we might as well not even bother."

He held up his hands. "I understand. I'll find someone else, someone better, and I'll make sure he's kind," he said, quickly. "I promise you'll be more pleased next time."

She wasn't confident he could find someone for her, but what other choice did she have? She refused to admit defeat. So instead of arguing, she sighed. "All right. I'll trust you. But the next meeting won't be over a meal. I want to be able to leave the second I decide he isn't a good fit."

"That's fair," he quickly agreed. "Besides, that will lessen the time needed for each introduction. Perhaps I could arrange for you to meet several men, one after another."

It sounded exhausting, but Zara would do anything, within reason, to stay and open her school. She'd been hopeful she'd be able to find someone suitable, but as the days passed, she'd become much less confident. "That'll be fine, if you can arrange it."

As if sensing her turn in mood, he stepped forward and placed a hand on her shoulder. "Don't worry, we'll find someone for you."

Confusion flared within her as she glanced up into his eyes. He cared about her, she could see that. Just not enough to put himself forward. He probably only cared because he felt responsible for her situation.

She sighed. Thaddeus might find someone for her, but Zara didn't think that person would be the *right* someone. "I really hope so."

CHAPTER 7

After the disastrous meeting with Mr. Chesley, Thaddeus suggested the next meeting take place in the hotel lobby. That way if Zara enjoyed the man's company, she could suggest they move to the dining room and have lunch, and if not, she could easily escape.

But as he waited on the boardwalk outside the hotel to give Zara and Mr. Norton privacy, he was conflicted. Their introduction had gone smoothly, and Zara had seemed interested in the man.

Thaddeus had never taken the time to contemplate another man's appearance and debate whether or not a woman would find them handsome, but he had a feeling Mr. Norton would please Zara both in looks and temperament. He'd spoken briefly with him and found him to be kind and considerate. He was also extremely wealthy, which was a necessity in Thaddeus' mind. Even if it was a lower priority for Zara, he wouldn't allow her to suffer in that way. As far as Thaddeus could see, they would be a good match.

He frowned. Why then didn't he feel more pleased about it? This was exactly what he needed to do to make amends.

He'd harmed Zara, regardless of his intention, and this was his restitution. He'd found someone who could take care of her and would make her happy.

It didn't matter if *he* was happy. Thaddeus didn't deserve to be happy in this scenario.

He kicked a pebble resting on a board by his foot. He needed to be happy for her and whoever she ended up marrying. Because that man wouldn't be him. No matter how much he'd come to care for her, no matter how much he longed for her to be his, it wasn't meant to be.

He had nothing to offer her. Not really. He barely had enough money to keep up his modest luxuries. There wasn't enough to buy her a proper wardrobe, let alone a home. Plus, he'd deceived her.

He wasn't worthy of her. Mr. Norton would be a good match for her, and Thaddeus would move on with his life. In a few more minutes he'd peer into the foyer to confirm they'd moved to the dining room. After that, he could grab a quick bite to eat. There was a new bakery that had just opened, and he knew he could quickly get a sandwich there.

But before he got the chance, the hotel door swung open and Zara stomped out.

"Zara, what's wrong? Where's Mr. Norton?" He glanced past her shoulder to see if the man was following her. Perhaps they wanted to eat elsewhere?

Her hands went to her hips, and she blew a tendril of hair from her face. "Did you even ask these men any screening questions before sending them to me?"

Thaddeus paused, thinking over what could have possibly gone wrong. "I spoke with him," he said slowly. "He's kind, wants a wife, and genuinely seemed to care for and appreciate women."

She tapped her foot. "Did you, by chance, ask Mr. Norton if he had a problem with his wife working?"

"No. He does?" The thought boggled Thaddeus' mind. "Why on earth would he have a problem with that?"

She held up her hands. "He wants a wife who will stay home, have lots of children, and take care of the house."

"And that's not you?"

"*No.* At least not right away. I'm not saying I don't want children. I do. Hopefully, several of them." She let out a frustrated breath. "The point is, I want to open a school. Right now, that's most important to me, what I've always dreamed of doing. It's the point to all of this."

"I understand." He hadn't even thought about asking such a thing. He'd assumed any man would be so pleased with Zara that it wouldn't matter if she opened a school or not. Apparently, he'd been wrong.

To him, Zara was perfection. Any man would be a fool to reject her for any reason. "I'll ask more questions next time. In fact, why don't you give me a list of questions and answers? You won't need to meet anyone else unless they fit your criteria. Would that help?"

She nodded reluctantly. "It would. Truthfully, I didn't think it would be this difficult."

Neither did he. "I'm sorry it's taking so long."

She shrugged. "I guess I should have expected it. Marriage isn't easy. I'm looking for someone to spend the rest of my life with, and I shouldn't rush into it with just anyone, should I?"

She looked to him for an answer, but he didn't have one. The thought of marrying a complete stranger was abhorrent. He had always thought he would eventually find someone to settle down with, but in his mind, it had been to someone he loved.

The woman in his mind was one who fascinated him, who brought him to life. Someone whose smile lit his world. She would be the first person he thought about in the morning and the last person he kissed before falling asleep. He hadn't known what she'd look like or where she'd come from, but he'd known those things.

He stilled as he watched her, admiring the way those depthless brown eyes looked at him. Dread settled in his gut as realization dawned.

The woman who had always been faceless before, suddenly wasn't. In that blank space was rich brown hair, chocolate eyes, and a keen mind.

Zara.

His heart skipped a beat, refusing to acknowledge what it meant. He couldn't possibly be in love with her. He desired her, cared what happened to her, but he hadn't known the depth of his feelings.

He'd come to know her, respect her, and appreciate her. He loved her laugh, the way her eyes sparkled when she was amused. He loved when she talked about Greek mythology, the way she brimmed with passion as she spoke about all the things she wanted to teach her students.

He'd been looking for someone to marry her, to help her get what she wanted, but he hadn't truly been looking for someone who would love her for who she was. But he knew one thing. He could look for the rest of his life, and he wouldn't find anyone who appreciated her as he did.

Feelings continued to blossom within him, and he knew he had to tell her, even though he didn't deserve her. If she rejected him, that was her choice, but he had to say something. "Zara—"

"I need someone I can trust," she said, as if realization hit. "Someone who isn't going to lie to me, who isn't going to try to control me. Someone I can depend on. Someone who will do what they say." She frowned and shook her head. "You know, I don't think I've come across anyone like that since coming here."

Thaddeus snapped his mouth shut and swallowed the

words which had almost come out. He tried thinking of a way to refute her words, but he couldn't. She was right. He'd lied to her, deceived her, had gotten her into this mess in the first place. She deserved someone so much better than him, and they both knew it.

But even with that knowledge, there was a selfish part of him that wanted to take her for himself, regardless of what she'd said. He wanted her more than he'd ever wanted anything in his life—even his mine—but because of that, he also wanted what was best for her.

But he was done being selfish. His selfish, careless attitude had hurt her enough.

He cleared his throat. "The next person I find will be everything you want. I'll make sure he's honest, kind, and will appreciate both you and your goals for the future. Unless he's everything on your list, you won't meet him."

She must have sensed something was wrong because she studied him again. But he held his face impassive. He wouldn't make this harder on her by throwing himself at her feet.

Finally, she relaxed her stare. "All right. We'll try *one* more match. But if the next one isn't a good fit, I'll take it as a sign it's time to go back home," she said, looking exhausted.

He nodded briskly, hoping the no nonsense gesture would keep him from revealing his true feelings. "This is going to work."

She looked at him again, but what he saw there tore at his heart.

She didn't believe him.

CHAPTER 8

I f Zara focused on finding a husband for one more minute, she was going to scream. It had completely dominated her every thought since coming to town, and she'd reached her limit.

She'd heard there was a library in the hotel, but hadn't ventured there yet. She'd been too busy to lose herself in books. Right now, that's exactly what she needed.

An escape.

She left her room and wandered through the hotel. She knew it was tucked somewhere off the main area but couldn't find it.

She glanced across the lobby and located one of the hotel employees. The man was speaking with a group of four women, so Zara felt comfortable approaching them. A few of the women laughed, and one with long, inky black hair and the bluest eyes Zara had ever seen teased another one.

The group laughed again.

As Zara approached, she caught the eye of the woman with pinned up, honey blonde hair, and Zara smiled in greet‑

ing. "Forgive me for interrupting, but I was hoping someone could point me to the library."

The hotel worker smiled regretfully. "Unfortunately, the library is closed for a private event, but it will reopen in three hours."

Her shoulders deflated. She was hoping to look through the books, but she could reread one in her own collection. "All right. Thank you."

She was about to turn away, when the woman with blonde hair stopped her. "Forgive me for being forward, but are you Miss Wigg?"

Zara turned back around, and the group of women looked at her curiously. "I am."

One of the other ladies with light brown hair smiled warmly, and Zara was instantly put at ease. "We've been hoping to meet you, but it never seemed like the right time. I'm Clara Morrison, the sheriff's wife. This is Juliette MacAllister," she said, introducing the woman next to her with dark hair and eyes and the palest skin Zara had ever seen. She gestured to the next woman. "Violet Thornton."

The woman's icy blue eyes studied her for a moment before she smiled. "Lovely to meet you."

"And," Clara continued, gesturing to the woman with honey blond hair, "this is Willow Winthrop."

Willow's last name gave Zara pause. "Winthrop?"

Violet snorted with amusement, but it was Willow who answered. "Yes. I'm married to Rhys Winthrop. He owns the hotel."

"Oh." Even though the women wore luxurious dresses, for a moment, Zara thought they could become her friends. But if one of them was married to a hotel magnate, that was unlikely. She cleared her throat. "It's lovely to meet you." She nodded politely.

Clara stepped forward, understanding and kindness in her

eyes. "Don't be intimidated. We might look fancy, but we're just like you."

Willow and Juliette nodded, and Violet shrugged in easy agreement. Still, Zara wasn't so sure.

But before she could say anything, Willow looked to the others and smiled at her. "We were just about to take tea in the library. We'd love it if you joined us."

Her eyes flew to the other women. They couldn't possibly want that. "That's very kind of you, but I couldn't impose."

Juliette smiled at her. "We'd like to get to know you. Besides, no woman looking for a library should be turned away." She grinned.

Violet rolled her eyes playfully. "And Juliette would know. She has an extensive collection, and you can usually find her nose in a book."

Juliette raised a brow. "It's true. I won't bother denying it." She looked at Zara, intrigued. "Do you enjoy reading?"

They all seemed interested in her answer. She cleared her throat. "I do. In fact, I'm hoping to open a school."

All eyes lit with interest. "A school? Here in Promise Creek?" Clara asked, excitedly.

Zara nodded. "That's my hope. Although, it's a bit complicated."

"You *must* join us then. We'd love to talk to you about it," Willow said.

At the women's encouraging looks, Zara relented. "If you're sure I'm not imposing."

"Absolutely not." Willow looked toward the hotel employee they'd been speaking with. "We'll be in the library. Please make the necessary arrangements now that we have an extra person."

"Of course, Mrs. Winthrop." The worker nodded respectfully and went to do as asked.

The women chatted amiably as they made their way

through a back door and down the hall. Zara knew she wouldn't have been able to find it on her own. "Isn't this an employee's only section of the hotel?" They walked into the library, and the familiar smell of dusty books set her at ease.

Willow gestured for them to sit in the comfortable lounge chairs. "At one point, this room wasn't open to the public, but when Rhys took over the hotel, he made it available for everyone."

It made sense. Books were expensive, and as she looked around the room, surprised by the total number of texts, she could understand why the previous owners had wanted to protect it. "That was very generous of Mr. Winthrop to share such a treasure."

Juliette beamed at her. "That's just what I thought as well."

Violet snorted her amusement. "That's because you benefit from it."

"Of course," she said, playfully sparring back. "But in any case, I'm sure Willow would've let me borrow as many books as I wanted."

Willow held up her hands with a laugh. "Don't involve me in this." She looked over at Zara. "You have to forgive us. We used to live together."

Zara glanced over the four women. They looked nothing alike. "Are you sisters?"

They laughed. "In a way," Clara said. "We were all mail-order brides for the same man."

Zara's mouth fell open, and the women chuckled at her shock. "One man ordered four mail-order brides?"

"Actually, he ordered ten," Violet said, dryly.

Ten mail-order brides for one man? Who ever heard of such a thing? "And I thought my situation was bad," she said. But when the others looked at her curiously, she berated herself.

They were seated comfortably in a circle, with a small table in front of them where the tea would go, so it was easy for each of them to look at her. And all eyes were *definitely* on her.

Willow cleared her throat. "Forgive me for overstepping, but if I may ask, how did you get to Promise Creek? Are you a mail-order bride?"

Zara would've assumed the details of her arrival would have spread like wildfire in a town this size, but apparently they hadn't. "You mean you haven't heard?"

The women shook their heads, and Juliette said, "We heard you're looking for a husband, but we haven't heard much else."

Of course, they would've heard that. The entire town knew about her search. It was something she should be embarrassed over, but she couldn't bring herself to care any longer. "I am looking for a husband. That's part of my problem with the school. But originally, I came as a mail-order bride."

"And something went wrong, didn't it?" Violet didn't sound at all surprised.

Zara nodded. "Exactly. I'd written someone. Someone who I thought was perfect." She couldn't help the bitter tinge in her voice, and the women looked at her empathetically.

"What happened?" Clara prompted.

Zara held up her hands. What *hadn't* gone wrong? "He wasn't who he said he was. Literally."

Willow frowned. "What do you mean?"

"Well, apparently, the man who sent for me thought it would be a good idea to have someone else write the letters."

Juliette gasped. "He didn't!"

Zara nodded sorrowfully. "He did. And the problem was... he seemed perfect." She shrugged. "Perfect for me anyway."

"How so?"

Zara wasn't sure who had asked that, but she answered anyway. "We have the same interests. He seemed to understand me, my love for Greek mythology and history. My desire to open a school." She quickly explained the situation with Wiggie and the other women from the orphanage who were going across the country to start schools. "But it turned out the man I was supposed to marry wasn't anything like that. It was the person writing the letters who attracted me."

Violet frowned. "What happened to the man writing the letters?"

"That's...complicated." She wondered how much she should say, then decided just to be honest. "He's wonderful, actually. He feels terrible about how everything turned out and is trying to help me. You see, it's imperative I marry. If not, Wiggie won't give me the funds to start a school."

All four gasped.

"That can't be."

"There has to be another way!"

"You shouldn't have to marry anyone you don't love!"

Regardless of the severity of their conversation, a chuckled escaped Zara. "Thank you for coming to my defense. But the truth is, my guardian gave me an ultimatum. I have two weeks to marry, or I have to return home and find another mail-order groom."

Juliette shook her head as if she couldn't understand such a thing. "But what about the school here?"

"I wouldn't be able to start one. I'd be opening it wherever my future mail-order groom lived."

The gravity of the situation seemed to take over the tone of the room, and the women fell silent. Finally, they looked at each other. "You know, there might be another way for you to stay and start your school."

Zara didn't understand. "How?" She frowned. "Unless I

marry, I won't have the money to start it. Even if I used a different building, the supplies are expensive."

Violet waved her hand in the air. "The expenses aren't a problem."

Clara nodded. "Violet's right. I don't know if you're aware or not, but the town started out as a mining camp. In the last year especially, the town has grown and will continue to grow. More families are coming, more children. We need a school. I'm sure you've heard there are many wealthy men here who made their fortunes mining."

"And women," Willow added with a wink.

Clara laughed. "And women. The man who duped us all into coming here, died three days before we arrived. In exchange for staying, the town gave us his house and mine. The mine at the time didn't pay very much, but it did in the end."

Zara had a hard time imagining that. "That's amazing."

Violet smirked. "I don't think anyone was more surprised than we were." The others laughed in agreement.

Clara shook her head. "What I'm saying is that if you'd like to stay, we can help you. We'll help you open your school, and you won't need any outside money to do it. The town will provide that."

Zara reeled at their generosity. "Thank you. I'm stunned." She shook her head as if trying to process what they were telling her. "But what about everything else? How will I get paid? Where will I live? There's so many other things to consider."

Violet swatted her hand through the air. "None of those things will be an issue. I'm sure the town would pay your salary and lodging. If not, I can think of a few places for you to stay." A look passed between the women, and they laughed again.

At her confused look, Juliette explained, "We still have

the house from Crazy Ivan, the man who brought us all here," she explained. "It's currently being rented, but it would be no problem for you to stay there as well until something more permanent could be arranged."

Zara looked at each of the women. "I don't know what to say. This has completely taken me by surprise."

Willow placed a hand on her arm. "We understand. It's a lot to take in. The choice, of course, is yours. But please know you don't have to get married. We won't require that. We also won't stop you from getting married, if that's what you want. Truly, the choice will be yours."

She wanted to pounce on the opportunity. They had solved all of her problems in a matter of minutes. She wouldn't have to worry about finding someone in the next week, or worry what her future would be like with that person or how she'd manage things. Everything would be taken care of.

But there was one issue.

Wiggie had been adamant she marry. Her guardian didn't feel it was safe to be out in the world as a young single woman. And with Zara being one of the youngest, Wiggie's concern had almost prevented her from going in the first place. Especially to a mining town like this.

This offer didn't require Wiggie's approval, though. Zara loved and respected her guardian, and didn't want to go against her wishes, but how could she turn this offer down? "Thank you for this opportunity. Truly, I'm amazed."

Violet's brow rose. "But you're not taking it?" The disbelief in her voice was evident.

"It's not that. I want to take it, to accept immediately. But..."

Understanding bloomed in Juliette's eyes. "But you're worried about your guardian, aren't you?"

Zara nodded, and she saw understanding brighten the other ladies' eyes.

Clara caught her attention. "You don't have to decide today. Take as much time as you want to consider your options. We completely understand if you choose to return home, but we would be delighted if you'd stay."

Willow agreed. "We would. Especially now that we're all married and having children." Willow looked to the others, and they laughed as if sharing a joke Zara didn't quite understand.

Then again, she did in a way. These women had been thrown into a difficult situation and had become like sisters. Just like the other girls in the foundling home had become Zara's family. Seeing what they had together caused an ache in her heart. The others had all gone their separate ways, spread throughout the country, but they still meant the world to her.

She wondered if she'd ever have that again.

They all looked at her with smiles on their faces, and she suddenly realized that if she stayed, she would. This town would embrace her, she knew it.

She just wished she knew what to do.

CHAPTER 9

The next day, Zara was still struggling with her choice. Thaddeus hadn't found her a match, and time was ticking away.

She'd stayed up all night, staring at the hotel ceiling. Finally, in the first light of dawn, she'd gotten out of bed, grabbed a piece of paper, and poured her heart out to Yetta.

Out of all the others from the orphanage, Yetta understood her the most. They'd shared a room for as long as Zara could remember. When some of the others thought Zara was flighty, Yetta had truly understood her. And she hoped just thinking of her would help Zara decide what to do. There was no way Yetta would receive her letter and be able to reply by Wiggie's deadline, but it helped to pour her heart out, to sift through her emotions.

When she was finished, her hands ink stained, and three pages filled, she knew what she had to do. She needed to wire Wiggie again and explain the current situation. It was possible Wiggie would support Zara taking the teaching position offered by the town.

Although Zara knew the likelihood was low, she still had to try. Doing anything else was dishonorable, and Zara refused to treat Wiggie in such a fashion after all she'd done for her.

After dressing, Zara glanced in the mirror, wincing at her image. The sleep deprivation was obvious, but that couldn't be helped. She needed to be at the telegraph office the moment they opened. There was no more time to waste.

Besides, what did it matter what she looked like?

She came down to the hotel lobby early and greeted some of the other guests before walking out the door. In a way, it felt like marching to the gallows, as dramatic as that sounded.

Regardless of what she hoped would happen, she knew Wiggie wouldn't support her taking the teaching position. Then Zara would have to make a choice, and her heart ached already because neither way felt right. She couldn't accept the position happily without Wiggie's consent, and if she returned home, refusing the position, she knew it would break her heart.

Fortunately, the Western Union representative was just opening the door when she got there. She sent her message quickly and concisely. Only giving the brief, bare facts.

Her fate would be decided within twenty-four hours.

She walked out of the telegraph office with a heavy heart and wandered back to the hotel. There wasn't much else to do today. No husband hunting. No interviewing candidates.

She walked in the door, deciding she might as well have breakfast since she was already downstairs.

"Zara?"

Of course he's here, she thought, glancing up at Thaddeus.

He looked at her with concern. "Is everything all right?" He glanced at the door she'd entered.

Is everything all right? No. It's not all right. Her life was turned upside down, her heart in turmoil. Did she still need to get married? Would she be going home? Nothing was certain except the uncertainty.

He stepped toward her and offered his arm. "Come with me," he said, softly.

She had no idea where he would take her, but it didn't matter. She slipped her arm through his, and he pulled her close. The feel of him, of being at his side and breathing his clean, spicy scent, eased her mind.

The muscles in his arm rippled, but she didn't think he'd done it on purpose. He seemed concerned for her, and she appreciated that.

As he walked across the foyer and through a side door, she realized he was leading her to the library. It would be empty this time of day, offering them privacy, but she didn't mind that. In fact, it sounded nice.

He ushered her into the familiar room, leaving the door cracked open for propriety's sake. The room was arranged differently today, the oversized chairs were pushed up against the sides of the room instead of in a circle like they'd been the day before.

Instead of offering her a seat, he whirled around and confronted her. "Tell me what happened."

She opened her mouth to speak but paused. His eyes bored into hers in earnest, like he cared, like he was torn up, knowing something was wrong.

He shouldn't feel that way for a stranger. Most people wouldn't be concerned with her life even if they'd played a hand in her difficulties. "Yesterday I had tea with several ladies from town. They offered to help me get my school started without a husband."

His eyes widened. "That's great news. That solves your problem then...doesn't it?" His uncertainty was clear.

"It solves part of the problem but leaves another."

He frowned. "I don't understand."

She didn't blame him. She lifted her hands and let them fall slowly. "It's everything I could want, except, I can't enjoy it if I go against Wiggie's wishes. She'd worry about me. She wanted me to have a husband to keep me safe. And if I accept this without her blessing, it will feel like tearing a piece of my heart out." She looked down to hide her expression. Her pain. All the turmoil within her rose to the surface, and her lips shook.

"Zara," he said tenderly, stepping toward her. He slowly tilted her chin up and stared into her tear-filled eyes. When one of the tears brimmed and slowly rolled down her cheek, he wiped it away with his thumb, his face pinching as though he were the one in pain. "Don't cry," he said hoarsely.

She lifted a hand and gripped his wrist, just holding him there. Closing her eyes, a few tears escaped before she opened them again. "I'm sorry. I just wish it wasn't so hard."

He brought his other hand up to her neck, cradling her. "What can I do? How can I help you?"

His voice, so tender, slashed her inside, and she didn't bother denying the truth that stretched between them. She loved him, wanted him, more than she had anyone else in her life. "Kiss me," she whispered. He stilled next to her, and she slowly brought her gaze to his. "Kiss me."

His fingers tensed on her face and neck, and she could see the debate raging over his features. He wanted this just as much as she did. But he still didn't make a move.

She leaned forward, brushing her lips softly over his. She gently pulled back. "I need you," she said honestly.

He groaned, and as if her words had dissolved the spell that had held him frozen, he moved his hand from her neck down to her waist, wrapping his arm securely around her. She gasped as he pulled her closer, his breath heavy and warm against her cheek.

He searched her eyes again, desire and disbelief mixing in his. "I shouldn't," he said, and a spike of disappointment shot through her. Then he shook his head. "I shouldn't, but I must."

Her stomach fluttered. But instead of placing his lips on her mouth, he leaned forward, angling his head to brush a kiss along her neck, breathing in her scent. His small wafts of breath shot tingles through her.

She moaned softly, overwhelmed with her body's response. He hardly touched her, but every nerve ending sparked with desire.

He moved back up, kissing close to her hairline, and her eyes rolled back in her head—it was then she realized he'd paused.

She opened her eyes slowly, meeting his heated gaze.

His eyes searched hers. "Are you certain?"

She brought her hands up to his arms and ran her palms up over his biceps to his shoulders. "More than anything. I need this. I need *you*."

He groaned and squeezed her before adjusting her head, turning it just slightly as he leaned toward her.

Her eyes fluttered closed, and, unable to stand the wait a moment longer, she lifted to her toes, bringing her mouth to his.

The full contact jolted her body. She gasped, and it was like that one sound triggered something in him. He squeezed her closer and dipped his tongue inside to taste.

Sounds exploded around her. Desire raced through her, and she gasped for air. Her body was hot and cold at the same time, but she relished the feeling.

This moment, the way he made her feel, was what she'd been waiting for her whole life. It was what she'd read about, dreamed about. She'd known it was real, regardless of what everyone else had said.

And she never wanted to let it go.

She hugged him closer to her, running her hands from his shoulders to his neck, and into his hair. His kiss became more aggressive, and she kissed him fiercely in return.

She strained closer, needing more as they moved together, breathed together.

But abruptly, he pulled from her. His eyes were wild, and he kissed her once more as if he couldn't help himself, then he tucked her in tightly against him, just holding her.

She felt as though her body had shattered and come back together stronger, fused with his.

They stood in each other's arms, their breaths moving in unison. Her head rested against his chest, and she heard his heart beating against his ribs. It thrilled her that she'd done that to him.

That they brought that out in each other.

Neither spoke for several minutes, but finally he shifted, and she reluctantly released him.

She looked at him with new eyes. He was what she wanted. She didn't care how they'd met, how things had started out between them. She knew he was a good man, one who had helped her when he hadn't needed to, someone who'd been there for her.

He'd cared for her every step of the way, and somewhere in there, she'd fallen irrevocably in love with him. She opened her mouth to speak, to confess how she felt and explain the feelings coursing through her.

"I'm sorry," he said gruffly before she could say anything.

She paused, his words disorienting her. "You're sorry?"

He looked away, and her stomach dropped. *He doesn't feel the same way*, she realized.

"That shouldn't have happened."

She swallowed hard, trying to guard against the hurt, but it sliced deep. "I wanted that to happen. That's why I asked you to do it."

Haunted eyes met hers. Eyes filled with regret. "I still shouldn't have done it."

"Why?" she asked, swallowing her pride. Her need to know overrode everything else.

He ran a hand through his hair. "Because I have nothing to offer you. Zara, I care about you. I won't deny that."

Her heart raced, and she stepped forward to touch him, but he flinched. She lowered her hand. "I don't understand. If you care about me—"

"I *do*. So much it's eating at me." He brought a fist to his stomach. "But because I care about you, I won't saddle you with my life and what it brings."

She still had no idea what he was talking about. "What if I like your life?"

He shook his head. "You don't understand." He gripped his coat lapels. "I might look successful, but I'm only a few days from being thrown out of the hotel." She frowned at his confession, and he nodded. "It's true. I haven't made my fortune like some of the other men in town. I can't provide for you. I can't give you a home, clothes, anything. At least not until my mine pays out."

She wanted to reach out again but knew he wouldn't accept it. "I don't care about any of that. You know how I grew up. I don't care about those things."

His jaw tightened. "But I do. The life I live is uncertain. I would never do that to someone I care about." His eyes met hers again, and she could see the determination there, the inflexibility.

Frustration wove through her. "So, you'd rather see me go to someone else?"

He winced. "No. But I won't saddle you with this life."

She didn't know what to do, what to say to convince him.

"Do you still need to marry right away? If the town is willing to help you set up a school, I don't see a problem with waiting."

She floundered, unable to process his words. She tried to understand his reasoning. "I don't know if I can accept their offer."

"Why?"

"Because doing so will go against the woman who raised me." She shook her head, refusing to allow tears to fill her eyes again. "After all she's done for me, I can't dishonor her like that."

He took a step forward, his expression wild. "But what about you? What about what *you* want? Don't tell me you want to return home, because I know that's not true."

"Of course not!" The words burst from her in a rush. "I want to stay here. I want to stay with you!"

He shook his head, denying her. "You don't know what that would mean."

She threw her hands up. He wasn't hearing anything she said. "I *do* know what it would mean," she countered. "I know life would be uncertain, that things could go sideways at a moment's notice. But what I *also* know," she said, looking into his eyes, begging him to truly hear her, "is that you'd never let anything happen to me."

He winced as if in physical pain and turned from her. It was then she realized she wasn't going to get through to him. "It's possible Wiggie will agree to you staying here without being married."

Her shoulders slumped. "Anything is possible. But it's highly unlikely. I'm the youngest, and she worried about me being vulnerable. She made that very clear before I left."

He shook his head as if the whole thing were impossible, and she was starting to see that it was. It was impossible for them to be together because he couldn't accept that she was willing to take risks to be with him.

Nothing would change his mind.

CHAPTER 10

Darkness licked at Thaddeus' heels. And while that hadn't bothered him in the past, it wasn't the lack of light in his mine that haunted him. It was the darkness in his mind.

He heaved his pickax into a stubborn rock, the mass holding steady. It was getting late, and he'd been in the mine since leaving Zara yesterday. But still he pressed forward, digging, working, as if physical exertion would ease his heart.

The dim lantern he worked with cast shadows on the wall like demons. This was the hellish existence he'd spoken to her of. He might look successful, but his life wasn't easy, and it certainly wasn't stable. This was why he refused to join their lives together.

He attacked the rock with renewed energy.

If only she could wait. If only she'd take the position the town had offered her, go against the wishes of the woman who'd raised her. It was selfish of him, but he still desired it.

He was close to the mother lode. He knew it. The gold was there, he could feel it just beneath the surface, but he wasn't willing to risk her, risk binding their lives together without proof. How could he do that to someone he loved?

And he *did* love her. So much he ached with want.

Kissing her, holding her, knowing she wanted him just as much, had almost broken him. But he hadn't pushed her away for his sake. It'd been for hers. Because he cared for her, he put her first.

I did the right thing. There was nothing else I could do.

He'd said those same things to himself over and over, but it didn't ease his pain. Or the pain it had caused her.

He still saw the flash of anguish on her features when she realized he'd denied her. Still, she looked at him, the person who had wounded her so deeply.

She would forgive him...wouldn't she?

His pickax slowed, as realization dawned. She might not wait. From everything she'd said, it was likely she wouldn't. She needed to marry or to return home. Those were the only two options she felt were acceptable, and he hadn't offered himself.

They loved each other, but which would be worse? If they married and lived like beggars, or if she married someone she didn't love who had money? Without a doubt, he would remain alone the rest of his life if she did. He'd gone his entire lifetime without feeling this way, and he knew he'd never feel it again.

Was he willing to risk losing Zara? All because his mine hadn't paid out?

If he were honest with himself, he knew he'd do whatever he had to in order to provide for her. If the mine failed, he would take another job to support them or strike another claim. He could make sure she never did without. But he'd never be able to give her the things she so deserved, the wealth he wanted to offer her.

He wanted to shower her with expensive clothing, jewels,

luxury in every step she took. But what he hadn't considered before was if Zara wanted those things for herself.

He swore and tossed the ax.

He could lose her. He could've lost her already.

Regret filled him as he thought of how his life could play out without her. It was unbearable, and he could only imagine how Zara felt. He'd rejected her, had told her a fortune was worth more than their feelings for each other.

And then he left her alone for over a day.

He reached into the pouch where he collected small scraps of gold from his mine and pulled out the pittance he'd found. It was enough to make a ring, enough to start a life.

Enough for a promise—if she'd have him.

He'd been a fool, and he hoped she would forgive him. Everything he'd learned about her, everything he knew, told him she would, but he wouldn't take that for granted.

This wasn't the first time he'd messed up. Writing her letters under a different name, deceiving her, had been wrong. But what he'd done to her in the library, walking away, he hoped it wasn't unforgivable.

He picked his ax off the floor and twirled it in his hands. He just wished he had more to give. But maybe his love could be enough.

His decision made, the burden eased from his heart. He loved her, wanted to marry her, and wanted to spend the rest of his life with her.

All he had to do was ask.

Excitement bubbled through him as he imagined what she'd say, how she'd react.

With more force than intended, he buried his ax in the rock and pulled. A groan followed by a cracking sound froze him in place.

His heart raced as he listened to smaller cracks, realizing what it meant. When the beam closest to him fractured, he grabbed his lantern and lunged forward—hoping, praying, the tunnel would hold long enough for him to get out.

Dust enveloped him. Rocks fell from the ceiling.

And the last thing he saw was a flash of thick, solid gold.

❧

WIGGIE'S LETTER ARRIVED A DAY AND HALF AFTER ZARA'S confrontation with Thaddeus. Zara hadn't seen or heard from him since, but she wasn't surprised.

He doesn't want me.

It still hurt, just thinking about it. But she had to accept it. He wasn't willing to take a chance, to risk living in poverty, and join their lives together. Why couldn't he understand she didn't need wealth? She'd come from nothing, and she hadn't come to Promise Creek hoping to marry a rich man. She'd come hoping for love and to start a school.

Both dreams seemed impossible now.

She shook her head as her eyes filled with tears. She refused to let any drop. She'd cried enough. It was time to buck up and make her decision.

She sat in the bedside chair in her room, staring at Wiggie's unopened message. She wondered what Wiggie had said, how she'd reacted. But as she ran scenarios through her mind, Zara realized it didn't matter.

She was an adult and had gone out into the world. She would always love Wiggie and respect her. But Wiggie had raised her to be an independent, intelligent woman.

Yes, she was young. She didn't deny that. But she was wise. Much more than her years would suggest. And in the time since Thaddeus had left, she had also realized one important truth.

She wanted her school and she wanted love more than she wanted Wiggie's approval.

She didn't know if she could wait for Thaddeus to strike it rich, or if he would ever be satisfied with his place in life, and she refused to put her life on hold.

And while she believed she would never love as fiercely again, it was possible for her to form an attachment with someone else. She could marry another and find contentment. And with the offer from the town, finding love was a possibility. She didn't need to marry immediately *or* return East.

She could stay here, start her school, and find a man who would love and respect her and share his life with her.

And with or without Wiggie's blessing, that's what Zara wanted. It was her life, her choice, and she hoped that no matter how Wiggie felt, she'd understand.

She jumped from her chair, unable to wait a moment longer before speaking with Thaddeus. If she had to, she'd go directly to his room.

She marched out the door, down to the front desk, determined to do whatever she needed to get to Thaddeus.

The clerk beamed when he saw her. "Good morning, Miss Wigg. What can I do for you?"

"This may seem like a strange request, but I was hoping you could tell me which room Mr. Gray is staying in. It's imperative I speak to him at once."

The man's eyes darted to the side. "I'm sorry, Miss Wigg, but we don't give out that information."

She wasn't surprised. "I understand the policy. But again, it's very important I speak with him without delay."

"I'm sorry. Even in an emergency, I can't give out those details."

Her shoulders deflated, but she refused to be defeated. Even if she had to sit in the lobby for the rest of the day. "Is there anything you can do?"

His eyes softened at her plea. "I could take a letter to his room," he said, but before she could get enthusiastic, he held up his hand. "But it wouldn't do you any good. I haven't seen him come in or out of the hotel in two days."

She frowned. "Two days? Are you certain? Is that common for him?"

The man shook his head. "No. I know he works in his mine, but he sleeps in the hotel every night. This is the first time he has stayed away."

"Thank you," she said hollowly and turned slowly away from the desk. What did that mean? He hadn't checked out. If he had, she was certain the clerk would've mentioned it.

But if he was still staying at the hotel, where was he? They'd had an argument, but it wasn't anything that should keep him from his bed. It wasn't as if they were sharing a room.

Could he be working? She nibbled her lower lip as she thought it over. If he was, had he truly not left his mine in two days?

Worry welled in her stomach. What if something had happened? What if he were hurt? No one would know. He'd shown her the way to his mine, but he'd made it clear it was a secret. Thaddeus didn't appear to have many close friends. She was probably the only one who knew where it was.

Should she ride out there on her own? If nothing was wrong, she would just make everything worse. Or, what if something *was* wrong and he needed help? There was no way she could lift him into a saddle on her own.

She couldn't decide what was worse: wondering if something was wrong, or being unable to make a choice.

But if there was even a small chance he was hurt, there wasn't really any other choice. She had to make sure he was all right. If she angered him, so be it.

She started walking toward the exit, formulating a plan, when she bumped into Clara Morrison, the sheriff's wife.

"Oh!" Clara said with a laugh. "Sorry. I was distracted. How are you, Zara?" After looking at Zara's face, she frowned. "What happened?"

Zara shook her head, trying to calm her heart. "Nothing. Well, maybe. I'm not sure."

"Tell me."

"Well...it's complicated."

Clara laughed softly. "Complicated is what I'm good at."

Zara hesitated. If she were wrong, she would look ridiculous, but if she was right and didn't get help, Thaddeus could die. Her hands fell to her sides. "I'm worried about Mr. Gray. He's been missing, and it's not usual for him."

Clara's head tilted to the side. "The Mr. Gray who's been helping you?"

"Yes."

Clara's eyes filled with understanding. "Why do you suspect something's wrong?"

"We had a disagreement a couple days ago," she said, shrugging. It had been so much more than that, but it didn't matter now. "He left and I thought he didn't want to see me. But I decided I needed to talk with him today, anyway. Then the man at the front desk told me he hasn't been back since we argued. He also mentioned Thaddeus has never skipped sleeping the night here."

Clara's brows pinched. "I see. That *is* concerning. Do you have any idea where he might be?"

"The only place I can think of is his mine."

"Do you know where it is? I know men try to keep it secret."

Zara nodded reluctantly. "He showed me. I think I could get back there on my own."

Clara's brow raised. "That says something about how he feels for you. He wouldn't have shown just anyone," she said softly.

Zara couldn't think about that right now. She blew out a breath. "I hope so." She shook her head. "I can figure that out later. But for now, I need a horse. I need to see if he's all right."

Before she could make for the door again, Clara reached out and stopped her. "If there's a problem, you're going to need help."

"I know. I just don't know who to ask. Who I can trust? If nothing's wrong and I've led all these people to his mine, he'll be upset."

"You can trust me. My husband's the sheriff. We know several men who would keep the mine's location a secret."

Zara didn't hesitate again. "How quickly can we get them?"

Clara squeezed Zara's arm. "Leave that to me." She nodded toward the door. "Go get a horse."

Zara didn't look back as she fled the hotel.

CHAPTER 11

Zara pushed her mount faster. With every bit of ground they covered, she felt more and more that something wasn't right.

She prayed she was wrong as she urged her horse faster. *I have to get to him.*

They were coming up to a fork in the trail, and the group looked to her. "Which way?" Sheriff Morrison called to her.

"Right!"

Without breaking form, the search party veered onto the correct path. After a few minutes, she worried they were in the wrong place, but then she saw a gnarled tree she'd noticed when Thaddeus had brought her.

Almost there. "Go left!"

No one slowed or wasted any time. They sensed something was off, too, and she was grateful for their help. She looked around at the faces who were becoming more familiar to her. She'd found friends and help faster than she ever thought possible.

The four women she'd had tea with, their husbands, and

several others, who she now realized were Ivan's other brides and their husbands, had all joined in to help find Thaddeus.

They had a bond she missed from her time in the orphanage and that she craved to have again. She might not share their history, but Zara knew she could have a close friendship with these women.

None of that would happen without Thaddeus, though. Without him, she didn't want to stay, didn't want to make a life here.

They flew into the small clearing with the mine's entrance, the sad little patch of grass still struggling where they'd had their picnic.

Everyone dismounted quickly.

Ronan, one of the husbands, pointed to the mine's entrance. "Let me go in first, make sure everything is sound before the rest of you follow."

Everyone agreed, and it made Zara feel more at ease that the rest of the men trusted Ronan with this task.

Clara came to her side and explained, "We hired Ronan to work our mine. He had his own claim that paid out as well. He knows what he's doing."

Zara placed her hands together and squeezed. "I just hope it doesn't take long."

Clara shook her head. "I'm no expert, but from what I understand, it's pretty easy to tell if there's been a collapse. Lots of dust in the air, debris. We'll know soon."

Her voice had turned grim, and Zara nodded.

Several of the others talked, forming plans about how best to rescue Thaddeus if he'd been caved in. The women gathered around her, murmuring reassuring thoughts. Zara appreciated the attempts, but until she saw Thaddeus with her own eyes, saw that he was well and whole, she wouldn't be all right.

Movement at the mouth of the mine drew her attention. It only took her a moment to realize it was Ronan, carrying a limp form over his shoulders. "Thaddeus!" Zara screamed and ran for him, terror blocking her throat.

Ronan gritted his teeth under the weight, but as several of the men converged, taking some of the burden, his features eased. "He's alive. Barely, but he's alive."

Zara's heart clenched, but hope filled her. *He's alive.* That was all that mattered. "What happened?" she asked, as several of the men hoisted Thaddeus over a saddle.

Ronan shook his head. "There was a minor breach and several large rocks fell. He has a head wound, but I don't know how bad the damage is. He's still breathing, so that's good." He whistled. "He's lucky. The whole thing could've gone, and he would've been buried."

She brought a hand to her stomach, sick at the thought of it. But it hadn't happened, and that's all that mattered. "Thank you. Thank you for coming."

He nodded then turned to the other men. "There's something else. It looks like he made a breakthrough. We'll need to keep an eye out until he wakes up."

Understanding lit in the men's eyes, but Zara was confused. She shook her head, looking from one to another. "A breakthrough? What does that mean?"

Ronan looked at her kindly. "It means he found the main vein. The mother lode. If people found out about it, there would be robbers in seconds."

Zara reeled at the information and what it meant. First and foremost, she felt joy. Thaddeus had done exactly as he'd hoped, he'd gotten everything he dreamed.

Then her eyes trailed to his unconscious form as several men tied him to the horse. He might not ever wake to see it.

She shook herself. She couldn't think like that. He *would*

wake up, he'd learn of his success, and everything was going to be fine.

She was sure of it.

"Asher and Tom, why don't you take first shift?"

A man who looked like he lived as a mountain man, albeit a far better groomed one, and another burly man with soot-stained clothes nodded in agreement before taking rifles out of their saddle bags.

One of the men with Thaddeus waved. "He's secure."

"Let's head back!" Ronan called out to the group, and there was a flurry of movement.

Zara ran for her horse, mounting in record speed. She watched as the men carefully and quickly guided the horse with Thaddeus over rough terrain, careful not to jostle him any more than necessary.

As they were about to turn the last corner, she glanced back at Thaddeus' mine, hoping and praying Thaddeus would live to see his dream come true.

***

FOR A WEEK, ZARA HARDLY LEFT THADDEUS' BEDSIDE. SHE prayed and grieved, even reprimanded him once, hoping it would rouse him.

But nothing had worked.

She sat in a chair beside him, holding his hand, and smoothed his hair back over his bandage. "You have to wake up," she said softly. "There's so much more I need to say. So much I need to tell you."

There was a soft knock at the door, but Zara didn't move away from Thaddeus. "Come in."

Willow entered, a frown on her face as she glanced at Thaddeus' still form. "Any change?" she asked, hovering in the doorway of his hotel room.

Zara shook her head. "Nothing." She looked down at his face, taking in the slopes and planes. He was so handsome. Even now, when he was pale and weak, he was still the most handsome man she'd ever seen.

But her heart ached. She wanted to see him well, talking, walking, thriving. "I wish there was something more we could do."

Willow moved next to her and sat in the other chair. They had decided to keep Thaddeus in his room in the hotel until he was well enough to decide to move out...or he passed.

It was more than generous for the Winthrops to allow such a thing. In the East, Zara knew they wouldn't have been as kind. But here in Promise Creek, they took care of each other.

"Is there really no one we can send for?" Willow asked, as if Zara's answer would've changed since yesterday.

Zara shook her head. "He never spoke of any family, and he never mentioned anyone in town he was close to."

Willow reached out and rested her hand on Zara's arm. She waited until Zara looked at her. "I meant for you, dear. Is there anyone I can contact for you?"

The question discombobulated her. Someone for her? She wasn't the one who needed help. Besides, who would she send for? Everyone she loved was unavailable. All the others were across the country, getting married and starting their schools. And Wiggie...Zara couldn't even think of her. Her guardian was ill and was surely already upset and worried that Zara hadn't responded to her latest telegram.

Her two-week deadline had passed, and with everything that had happened, she'd never sent a reply. She could only imagine what Wiggie thought, how disappointed she must be.

As if that were the final straw, a sob broke from Zara's chest. "I don't know what to do." Then another sob escaped her, and she did her best to choke it back. "I don't know what to do."

Willow moved closer to her, wrapping her arms around her. "It's all right. You're not alone. Just let it out."

Zara didn't want to. She wanted to stay strong, to hold it together, to be the strength Thaddeus needed to recover. But she couldn't stop it. Couldn't hold it back a moment longer.

The anguish that had built in her since coming to Promise Creek, erupted. Sobs wracked her body, and she heaved in breaths, unable to get enough air as the pain assaulted her.

She leaned forward, clinging to Thaddeus' hand, and Willow wrapped an arm around her, as if trying to hold her together through the storm.

She wouldn't be all right if Thaddeus died. She wouldn't recover and move on. She'd thought it possible to find another man to care for, possibly even to love, but now she knew that wouldn't happen. With a shattered heart, how could she come to care for someone else? How could a person recover from such grief enough to open their heart again?

Her hopes and dreams and grief melded together, trying to escape with her tears.

But as the storm cleared, and her breathing slowed, clarity filled her.

No matter what happened to Thaddeus, Zara would stay in Promise Creek. She might not get married and have a family of her own, but she would start the school. She would teach about the Greeks, about laughter, and even mining, along with the other subjects.

And she would never ever forget Thaddeus.

She sucked in a deep breath and leaned back, brushing her tears away. "Thank you for being here."

Willow gave her one more squeeze before releasing her. "Of course. You're not alone. No matter how it feels, you're not alone."

"I know. You, all of you, have shown me that. I can never repay your kindness, what you've done for me and Thaddeus. Thank you for being my friend and allowing me to stay in the hotel with him," she said, glancing at the man she loved. She took a deep breath and met Willow's eyes. "I wanted to let you know that if you're still looking for a teacher, I'd like the position."

Willow's eyes widened. "Are you sure? You don't have to decide now."

Zara nodded and sniffed. "I am. Regardless of anything else, it's what I want. Promise Creek has come to mean so much to me, has become my home in such a short amount of time. I want to stay."

"Of course. We'd love to have you."

Zara's next breath was shaky. "I'm not sure when I could start or when I'll be able to repay you for my stay here."

Willow waved her concern away. "We're happy to help you, and there's no charge for your room. And there's no rush with the school either. You can start whenever you're ready. If you'd like, a few of the ladies and myself can get things ready for you. We can order whatever you need."

Zara smoothed a hand over Thaddeus' blanket. "Thank you. That will help things get started once everything is decided for Thaddeus." She couldn't bring herself to say after he passed away. But with every day that crept by with no change, his situation looked dire. Still, she needed to keep hope.

"Zara, you should really take a break. I'll stay with him a bit while you're gone."

Zara knew Willow was right. She'd been taking her meals in Thaddeus' room, but she really needed to freshen up. She'd been wearing the same gown for two days. "All right. Thank you. I'll be back shortly."

Zara stood and Willow hugged her. She pulled back and

sat in the chair Zara had just vacated, saying, "Take as long as you need."

Zara nodded, but she had no intention of dawdling. She wanted to be by Thaddeus' side, good or bad.

CHAPTER 12

The first thing Thaddeus noticed upon waking was the pain. It was a dull throbbing ache at the front of his head that pulsed with each beat of his heart.

Next was the light. As he cracked his eyes open, it felt like looking into the sun. He clenched his eyelids shut, hoping to block out the brightness which only made his headache worse.

His throat was also dry, like he'd been wandering through the desert without a drop to drink.

What happened to me?

He held still, sorting through his thoughts, his memories, but they were a jumbled mess. Besides his head, the rest of his body felt fine. Sore, but otherwise unharmed.

He reached up with his arm to touch his head. He only lifted his hand a few inches before it fell back to the bed. He was aghast at the weakness he felt. The second attempt was successful, now that he knew what to expect. His fingers found a bandage wrapped around his forehead.

"Thaddeus?"

His voice had been called softly, and he wondered if it was real.

But then a soft hand covered his, and he breathed in the scent of sunshine and apples. "Zara," he tried to say, but no sound came out past the dryness of his throat.

"Thaddeus! You're awake!" Zara's voice cracked at the end. "Can you open your eyes? Are you in pain?"

His body rebelled at the thought of opening his eyes again, but he would do anything for her. It took a few attempts, but his eyes opened, and he took in her beautiful face. He could tell she'd been crying, that she hadn't been sleeping, but he'd never seen a more beautiful sight in his life.

Her eyes brimmed with fresh tears, and she smiled. "It's so good to see you." She placed a hand on his face, cradling his cheek. "I wasn't sure I ever would again."

"Wha—" His throat closed up against the word.

She frowned. "Is it your throat? I've been trying to spoon water into your mouth, but I'm sure it wasn't enough."

She reached behind her and grabbed a cup and spoon off the side table. "Here, allow me."

She proceeded to feed it to him gently, patiently. And with every moment that passed, all he wanted to do was tell her how much he loved her. How much he needed her.

After a few spoonfuls, she leaned back, her eyes apologetic. "I'm sorry. I don't want to give you too much in case it upsets your stomach."

He saw the logic in that, and while he was still thirsty, he needed to talk to her more than he needed water. "What happened?"

She frowned. "You don't remember?"

He shook his head slowly. "It's a little fuzzy."

"You were in your mine. A couple days after our argument, I realized how wrong I'd been. I went to find you, but the employees at the hotel said they hadn't seen you, and that it was strange for you."

Happiness and regret wove through him. He moved his hand, and she brought hers to his again. He squeezed. "I'm sorry for how that conversation went. I'm sorry you worried."

She shook her head. "There's nothing to apologize for. I understand why you feel the way you do. But none of that matters now."

"It doesn't?" he asked, even though he agreed with her. His memories from that night were quickly coming back. Before the cave in, he'd already decided that nothing mattered more than her.

Then he remembered the flash of gold right before he was knocked unconscious. He sucked in a breath, and with a burst of energy, he pushed himself up to sit.

Her eyes flared with concern, and she placed a hand on his shoulder. "You shouldn't tax yourself. Lie down."

He shook his head, ignoring the ache there, and his eyes latched onto hers. "The mine. Before I hit my head, I thought I saw gold. *Lots* of gold." He couldn't have imagined it, could he?

She still looked concerned. "You need to lie down. You've been unconscious for a week."

"I need to know, Zara. I'll worry otherwise. Did I imagine it?"

She looked at him for a moment and seemed to determine he was doing all right, regardless of the abrupt activity. She gave him a small smile then proceeded to shove pillows behind his back to support him.

Finally, she sat in the chair next to the bed and took his hand. "You didn't imagine it. Ronan said you hit the main vein. You're a wealthy man, Thaddeus."

Breath escaped his lungs. *I knew it.* He hadn't imagined it. Everything he'd worked for, everything he'd dreamed of, had come true. He was thrilled, overwhelmed—and yet none of that could compare with his feelings for Zara.

"Are you all right?" she asked when he hadn't responded. "Are you going into shock?"

He laughed then, the sound gravelly. "I *am* in shock, a little. I knew I was close to finding it, but I didn't expect to uncover it like that." He frowned, finally processing what Zara had said. "Did you say Ronan told you about it? Ronan Briggs? How does he know?"

She nodded and looked away guiltily. "When you were missing, I knew something was wrong, and I needed help. Clara and the sheriff helped me, along with a few others he said could be trusted."

Relief coursed through him. If Sawyer Morrison and Ronan Briggs were involved, Thaddeus knew his mine was safe.

"I'm sorry I broke your trust," she rushed to say. "I knew your mine's entrance was a secret, but I brought them anyway."

He squeezed her hand. "You did the right thing." He waited until she met his eyes. "You did the right thing," he said again, wanting to reassure her. "If you hadn't brought them, I'd probably be dead."

She bit her lip. "That's what the sheriff said as well."

He nodded slowly. "I'm assuming they're protecting the mine?"

"They are. They stationed two men there, rotating every six hours."

Gratitude overwhelmed him. He hadn't made close friends in town. He'd been too busy with work for such things, but still, when there was a need, men stepped in to fill it.

They'd protected what was his, and for that, he'd be forever in their debt.

"They said that, once you woke up, they'd talk to you about what you'd like done with the gold."

He waved that away. As important as it was, there was something much more important he needed to say. "Thank you for coming for me, for rescuing me. You could've left me there, but you didn't. I owe you my life."

She shook her head quickly. "It was nothing more than anyone else would've done."

"That isn't true. You could've still been angry with me, and happy to never see me again."

"No matter what happens, I'll never feel that way." She looked at him solemnly. "I want—"

He squeezed her hand, and she paused. "There's something I need to say."

"All right." She sounded like she was about to hear a jury's verdict.

He waited, gathering his thoughts. "Before the mine collapsed, before I saw the gold, I'd been working in there for hours." He let out another rough chuckle. "Over a day. It was stupid, but with how I felt inside, torn up over our conversation, it was the only way I knew to purge myself of that pain."

She lowered her head, but he reached over and lifted her chin. He wanted her eyes on him when he said this. "I was foolish, but please know that my desire to wait until I had my fortune was only because I felt you deserved better."

She shook her head. "No one is better than you."

"I realize that." He grinned ruefully. "Before the collapse, I realized I was a fool for asking you to wait. You're everything to me, everything I've always wanted. When I'm with you, I feel as though, for once, everything is right and good. That anything is possible. I've always dreamed big. No one who comes out West and strikes a claim is any different. But being with you, imagining our life together, is better than anything I could've hoped for." He stared into her eyes, willing her to understand. "I love you, Zara. I don't want to wait to be with you. And although it sounds crazy"—he chuckled—"I almost wish I hadn't found the gold, just so you'd know how much I really mean that."

Hope bloomed in her eyes. "Truly? Are you certain you won't change your mind? You *have* been in a coma."

When their laughter trickled off, he leaned toward her, placing his hand on the back of her neck to pull her closer. When their foreheads touched and her eyes shuddered closed, he whispered, "I've never been more sure of anything in my life. Please, Zara, marry me. Be my wife. My partner. We'll finish up my mine and open your school together. Nothing will keep us apart again."

"Yes," she said softly. "Yes. I'll marry you. I love you, Thaddeus."

Her words were like a balm to his soul, and joy filled him. He pulled her closer, sealing his lips to hers. His life to hers.

With every breath he took, every touch they shared, he felt the future spread out before them.

She pulled away softly. "Be careful. You shouldn't—"

"Overtax myself," he said, finishing for her. Before she could say anything else, he pulled her forward, and she let out a surprised cry as she toppled onto the bed beside him.

He turned toward her, so they lay facing each other, and snaked an arm around her waist, cradling her close. He didn't want to admit it, but he was exhausted. Still, he wanted her next to him.

He paused, allowing her the chance to move off the bed if she chose.

Instead, she smiled softly and cuddled closer.

He rested his cheek against the top of her head, inhaling her scent. He sighed, closing his eyes in contentment. For the first time in his life, everything was right. "I love you."

She wrapped an arm around his waist. "I love you, too."

She leaned back to look at him. "But if I have to, I'm going to tie you to this bed until you heal. If you ever scare me like this again, you're going to regret it."

"Yes, ma'am." He tipped an imaginary hat.

She laughed and swatted his arm before snuggling against him again. "When do you want to get married?"

"How soon are you going to let me out of this bed?"

A startled laugh fell from her lips. "As soon as possible."

He kissed the top of her head. "Then we'll marry as soon as you let me out of bed."

They lay like that for a long while, talking, laughing, kissing, and dreaming. Loving Zara and being loved in return was his greatest blessing. He was a very rich man indeed.

EPILOGUE

Zara walked through her schoolroom, checking over the children's desks when she noticed Albert's slate on top. She clucked her tongue, making a mental note to speak with him about treating school supplies with respect.

She wasn't upset with him, more amused. The boy seemed to have his head in the clouds. As a dreamer herself, she couldn't fault him for that. But she could teach him how to temper it, just as Wiggie had done all those years ago for her. Wiggie had never tried to quash that part of her. Instead, she had taught Zara discipline to go hand-in-hand with her dreams.

She'd always be grateful to her.

Thinking of the woman who'd raised her so lovingly, an ache formed in her heart.

Zara had been married for six months now. The school she'd dreamed about had been built quickly and efficiently, and was completely paid for by the town. But Wiggie's donation had gone a long way in providing the extras.

Zara would always be grateful Wiggie had chosen to trust

her when she'd failed to find a husband within the two-week deadline.

But that was Wiggie. She loved all her girls from the orphanage. No matter what they'd done, no matter how different their personalities, she loved each and every one of them. Zara couldn't imagine the world without her.

She put away Albert's slate and sunk into the boy's chair. This wasn't the time to mourn, but Zara wondered how much longer Wiggie would live. It was a miracle she'd survived this long with how dour her prognosis had been.

She shook her head and stood, refusing to wallow in grief for something that hadn't happened yet. When Wiggie passed, she'd mourn. Until then, she'd try to have hope.

Zara took a deep, calming breath. Besides, Thaddeus would be here any minute, and where they were going next was a place she wanted to enjoy to the fullest. The house they'd commissioned was finally finished.

It was hard to believe, but the day they'd looked forward to was here. They'd paid a premium to have it constructed quickly, but it was worth every penny. She thought of the four-bedroom, two-story home, it's full wraparound porch, and the fertile land it sat on at the base of a small hill ten minutes from town. It wasn't as grand as Thaddeus had wanted, but it was perfect.

She snorted. If it had been left to him, he would've built a palace to rival Zeus', just as he'd said when she first met him. She didn't want a palace, a place for others to see how grand they were. She wanted a home.

And that's exactly what Thaddeus had given her. A place where they could grow, could love, and where their children could play.

Unconsciously, she rubbed the growing bump in her lower stomach. When she noticed what she was doing, she looked down and spoke to her growing child. "You're going to love it, little one. There's room to play and grow, room to run around and explore."

There hadn't been much room in the orphanage, and while space would have been nice once in a while, what meant most to her were the other girls. Her family. The thought brought another ache about Wiggie.

She rubbed her belly again. "I promise, I'll try to give you plenty of brothers and sisters."

The door to the school opened, and Thaddeus stepped inside. Before he could say anything, she launched herself toward him, seeing his grin before he caught her in his arms.

He held her close and he chuckled. "I'm glad you're excited." He brushed a kiss across the top of her head, and his laugh muffled in her hair. "I'll admit, I'm barely containing myself."

She gave him an extra squeeze, then he pulled back and looked in her eyes. He smoothed a hand over her hair before cradling her cheek. "Is everything all right?" Worried, he glanced down at her stomach. "Are you well?"

Love rushed through her, and she brushed a soft kiss across his lips. "Yes. We're both doing just fine. It's a big day."

He smiled, and she loved seeing him so content. "An *exciting* day."

She rolled her eyes. "You're just happy to move out of the hotel."

He grinned. "Of course." But then he leaned forward and left a hot kiss on her neck and whispered, "But I'm also excited to fill our new home with children. And I plan on there being *many* more."

A shocked and delighted laugh escaped her as his hand rested over her stomach. She knew he was thrilled they were having a child, and he'd made certain to show her every day how much their baby meant to him. "I think we're off to a good start."

He nodded and placed a kiss on her lips. "Yes, we are. But it would be best if we didn't get rusty."

"Rusty?" What was he talking about?

"Yes. Making babies is a skilled job. We'll need to make sure to practice often so we'll be in top form when it's time to make another one."

A laugh erupted from her, and she playfully smacked his arm. "I don't think practicing is a problem for us."

He kissed her then, his lips meeting hers in a hot caress. He lingered, savoring her, drawing it out until some of her amusement faded, replaced by desire. Then he pulled back and looked her in the eyes. "And it never will be. I love you. I wish I could spend every moment of every day showing you just how much."

Her heart soared, and she wrapped her arms around his neck, pulling him forward. "Good. Because I wish for the same." She shook her head and let out a small laugh. "I always imagined what it would be like to be married, to be in love and be loved like this."

His brow quirked. "And is it like what you thought?"

She shook her head, but when he frowned, she grinned. "It's even better."

A smile bloomed on his face, and he hugged her close, slowly bringing his lips to hers, when a cane thumped on the floor behind them.

A mock-stern voice cut through the air. "Now, Zara, this behavior is quite inappropriate for the school room."

Shock filled her. Thaddeus was blocking her view of the doorway, but she knew that voice. It couldn't be—"Wiggie?"

Zara sprang to the side, shouting with joy as her beloved guardian came into view. Thaddeus stepped away and gently nudged her forward, realizing who the elderly lady was.

But Zara didn't need any nudging. She leapt forward,

encasing the woman in her arms. "Wiggie? Is it really you? What are you doing here?"

As her initial shock and excitement wore off, Zara remembered Wiggie's health and pulled back. Horrified, she looked for injuries after mauling the ill woman in her excitement. "I'm so sorry! Are you all right? Did I hurt you?"

Laughter twinkled in Wiggie's eyes. "I'm fine, dear. I'm happy to see you too." Her eyes looked beyond Zara to Thaddeus. "And is this your young man?"

Emotions flitted through her so rapidly she couldn't hold onto them. There was joy at seeing Wiggie again, but it was dampened by knowing it would most likely be the last time, before she succumbed to her illness. Wiggie would never see Zara's baby.

She didn't want to focus on that though. This was a happy moment, and she wanted to bask in that. So instead, she focused on Wiggie's question and turned toward Thaddeus. "Yes. This is my husband, Thaddeus."

With a warm smile, he stepped forward and took Wiggie's hand in his. "It's an honor to meet you, Madam Wigg."

Wiggie swatted away the formality. "Call me Wiggie. You married one of my girls, and that makes you family."

He grinned. "Wiggie, then."

Wiggie's eyes twinkled as she looked at Thaddeus. She inclined her head slightly toward Zara. "He's quite handsome, dear. You've done well for yourself."

"Wiggie!" Zara's jaw dropped open. "You know very well I didn't choose him for his looks!"

Wiggie winked. "Of course not. But it doesn't hurt."

Zara groaned, but Thaddeus laughed. "I like you, Wiggie."

The older woman nodded as if just deciding something. "I like you too. I approve of this union."

"It's a little late for that," Zara said, dryly.

Wiggie's eyes went to Zara's expanding middle. "Yes," she

said with amusement. "I do believe it is, but I'd like to give my blessing yet again."

Zara's heart clenched, and she couldn't stop herself from pulling Wiggie into another embrace. "Thank you. That means everything to me, to know you approve and support what I've done." She pulled away reluctantly. She wanted to continue hugging Wiggie, knowing it was only a matter of time until she couldn't do it any longer.

Wiggie smiled in acknowledgement before turning her gaze around the school room. "Looks mighty fancy in here. The town supports you," she said, pleased.

"They do," Zara agreed. "They're very supportive, both emotionally and financially."

"That's good then."

"But your donation went a long way as well. I'm grateful for that."

"I'm happy you were able to use it, dear." She walked to one of the desks and opened the top, glancing at the contents before moving on to look around the rest of the room.

Zara glanced at Thaddeus, and he shrugged.

Zara moved toward Wiggie again. "Wiggie, I'm so happy to see you, but why are you here?"

Wiggie turned back toward her, her brow raised. "Can't I visit you when I like?"

Zara huffed. "Of course. You know you're always welcome." She shifted on her feet, uncertain whether she should bring up her illness or not, but realized she couldn't avoid it. "I'm only concerned. Perhaps you shouldn't be traveling in your condition?"

"My condition?"

Was Wiggie really going to make her say it? "You're lucky you've lasted this long. I'd hate for you to tire yourself with all this traveling."

Wiggie laughed and wiggled her smooth, white eyebrows.

"My dear, I love you and the others dearly, but I thought you all would've figured it out by now."

Zara frowned. "Figured out what?"

"I'm not sick. I never have been."

Breath rushed from Zara's lungs, and her hands went to her hips. "You're *not*? Then why would you tell us such a thing? We all thought you were dying!"

She nodded wisely. "I know. As for you, you didn't need the prodding, but I knew the others might not have left, otherwise. Moving on, going West and starting your own schools, that's what you all needed. It's what I wanted for you. I'm sorry I had to deceive and worry you, but that just shows how great a person I raised."

Zara floundered, uncertain how to feel. She was elated Wiggie was well and that there wasn't cause to mourn. From the looks of her, she'd live for many years to come. But that didn't mean Zara would let her off so easy.

Zara narrowed her eyes. "I'm thrilled to hear it, but don't think you're going to get off easy after that. You scared us all half to death." Wiggie tried to look penitent, but couldn't quite pull it off. "Do the others know?"

"Some. But I'll let them know as I continue to visit all of you."

Zara's hands slid off her hips. "You mean you've visited some of the others already?"

Wiggie smiled indulgently. "Several settled closer to the orphanage than you, Zara."

She knew that, of course, but she was still so surprised. "So, you're really all right?" she asked again, needing to hear it one more time.

Wiggie stepped toward her and put a hand on her cheek. "Yes, dear. And with you all happily settled, I'm now able to fulfill one of my biggest dreams: to travel around and see the world."

A surprised gasp escaped Zara's lips, and Thaddeus chose then to come up next to her and wrap his arm around her. "That sounds like a grand adventure."

Another twinkle entered Wiggie's eyes. "It is. And it's only the beginning."

As Zara looked at Thaddeus, she thought the same thing. Life together was the grandest adventure, and with their love, a new home, and a baby on the way, she couldn't wait to see what else was in store.

*****

Thank you for reading The Alphabet Mail-Order Brides! I hope you enjoyed all the stories as much as I have. If you have a moment, please consider leaving a review for Zara's Zephyr or any of the other books in the series. They help other readers find books they might like, and they mean so much to authors.

If you missed one of the stories, you can find all the books in the series at
www.janelledaniels.com/alphabet-mail-order-brides.html

I also wanted to take a minute to thank you for being one of my readers! Because of you, I've been able to live my dreams. I can't thank you enough!

-Janelle Daniels

FREE DOWNLOAD

**Will Father Christmas bring
them their happily ever after?**

amazon kindle

★★★★★ 4.5 out of 5 stars

Get your free copy of A Christmas
Secret when you opt-in to the
Janelle Daniels Readers Club.
Get started here:

http://www.janelledaniels.com/claim-your-free-book.html

My Only Wish

Collaborations

Kitty: Bride of Hawaii (American Mail-Order Brides)

Falling for a Duke (Timeless Regency Collection)

Zara's Zephyr (The Alphabet Mail-Order Brides)

The Witches of Redwood Falls

The Witching Moon (The Witches of Redwood Falls – Book 1)

The Witches Craft (The Witches of Redwood Falls – Book 2)

Discover other titles by Janelle Daniels

www.JanelleDaniels.com

Connect with me online.

I love to hear from readers!

Facebook:

https://www.facebook.com/groups/411789749214006/

Pinterest:

http://pinterest.com/JDanielsRomance/boards/

Twitter:

https://twitter.com/_JanelleDaniels

ZARA'S ZEPHYR

Dream Cache Publishing

This is a work of fiction. Names, characters, places, and incidents either are products of the author's imagination or are used fictitiously. Any resemblance to actual events or locales or persons, living or dead, is entirely coincidental.

www.janelledaniels.com

Copyright © 2019 by Janelle Daniels

Cover Art © 2019 Erin Dameron-Hill

All rights reserved.

No part of this book may be reproduced in any form or by any electronic or mechanical means, including information storage and retrieval systems, without written permission from the author, except for the use of brief quotations in a book review.

www.ingramcontent.com/pod-product-compliance
Lightning Source LLC
Chambersburg PA
CBHW020414130626
46549CB00006B/2557